```
// ----------------------------------
----------------------------
a=href <return> prologue
            >
// -----------------------------------------------------
----------------------------
```

Even if you've never heard a gun go off before, you wouldn't mistake it. A rush of wind and blood. The sound of an impact more than the impact itself. People hear a car backfire and they startle, thinking: "was that a gunshot?" But nobody ever hears a real gunshot and says "was that a car?" You just *know*.

BANG. It's an explosive, guttural sound that comes from a place so deep I'm afraid to think about its origins. It is the most unpredictable sound I have ever heard and it has an unpredictable effect: I spring into action. I am off my feet and in the air hurling towards the shooter before I can say to myself: duck, you idiot.

Just to be clear this is not something I had ever imagined I would do. Not that being in a situation where I'd be hurling towards someone holding a gun ever occurred to me. I just wasn't the one who'd stick up for the kid getting beat up. I was the one who'd hide, worried that I'd be next. But in the context of this summer, I guess the unexpected is exactly what you'd expect. It's fitting, really, that I would be the one that somehow ends up getting caught in the crossfire. In the middle of this war of the houses that I happily participated in, maybe even instigated. It all makes sense. And here I am: seventeen-year-old Charlie Middle in the role of Mercutio. Five feet away and closing in on the familiar shape whose hand is on the trigger. I brace for the impact and try to tell myself to relax; I'm probably already dead. But the impact never comes.

I unclench my body and open my eyes, but seem to be frozen in mid-air. There's no noise. It's not that it's quiet; in fact I'm sure there are screams and groans and all sorts of chaos. But the sound is missing for me. Like it's been taken. My eyes alternate: I stare down the eyes of the shooter, then the barrel of the gun that's pointed right at me, then those eyes again. I could swim in those eyes they're so big and shocked. Regardless of how this works out, I'll know they obviously didn't mean to kill me. For whatever that's worth.

As if on cue, time lets go of the arrow it's drawn. My velocity returns. The inevitable impact comes, and with it another BANG, a flash, and a sudden, permanent pain.

The sky looks like a freshly paved road. Lying on my back in the grove behind my cousin Maisey's house, I still hear the gunshot ringing through the trees. Maybe it's been minutes, seconds, maybe less. I look up from the patch of Earth I occupy and think about the cost of the small patch of real estate beneath me. It's more than I have in my savings account. More than my parents have in theirs. Including my college fund. I can't feel my legs. I hear Joss scream for Maisey. It is the most awful sound… the sound of a heart breaking. I lay there, unable to move.

"Where are the stars," I mumble, as everything goes dark.

DISEMBODIED POETICS

http://such great heights/a novel/by chris cole

Published in the United States by Disembodied Poetics
PO Box 65 Lagunitas, CA 94938
http://suchgreatheights.cc

Cover: Sorenquist.Deviantart.com

Printed in USA | First Edition | 10 9 8 7 6 5 4 3 2 1

ISBN 978-0615819075

For Jake, Isabel and the muse.

CHAPTER ONE

"This might have been a horrible mistake," I mumbled to myself.

I was hurtling toward the ground from thirty thousand feet. I put my forehead against the oval window and thought that the land below looked as foreign as Afghanistan. *Going to California* by Led Zeppelin was the last song on the playlist my dad made for me. It was winding down and I hoped it would finish before I got that look from the stewardess that said, *turn it off.*

I pulled the crinkled ticket out of my pocket and stared at it:

> Middle, Charlie
> Minneapolis to Silicon Valley
> One Way

I had lucked, with a capital L, into a summer internship at a technology company called Retroverse—its name and its product a mystery to me even now. All I know is that everyone was fiending for gigs like this. Silicon Valley was the new Wall Street, the new Hollywood for that matter. And I'd be staying right at the heart of it.

I didn't realize at this point the nexus of power and money and lust that I was about to be thrust into. Nor what the cost of admission would be. My second cousin Maisey and her much older husband Reed Graft were still reputable people in my mind. Reed got me the intern gig, the only child of one of the founders of Silicon Valley from way back in the seventies, before the Internet. He and Maisey got married when she was just seventeen. That was kind of a red flag, if I'm being honest. But honesty is the privilege of an educated mind, as Reed would later tell me.

I was the last to leave my seat when we landed. Staring at the fastened tray table, I didn't want to battle the bodies bobbing their way up the aisle. Plus, I felt like as soon as I stepped off the plane there'd be no going back. I didn't want to go back. Or forward really. I wish there was a way to pause.

When I finally got out to the gate, a tall, bearded man in a black suit and matching sunglasses stood amidst the darting travelers. He looked like Will Smith, circa *Men In Black*, and he was holding a sign with my name on it.

I looked at him, confused. As soon as we locked eyes, he approached me. "Welcome, Mr. Middle," he said with a confident, cursory smile. "James."

"Charlie," I answered back.

James whisked up my bags, and ushered me toward the exit. As we made our way through the terminal I kept falling behind. Silicon Valley International was a brand new airport—a reinvention of the airport, really. Aside from the security stuff it was more like a high tech mall. There was a massive arcade complete with every old game you could imagine from when you were a kid to things that haven't even been released yet. There was even a movie theatre with a sensory depravation prototype. And an Apple Store, of course. There were all kinds of tech history strewn about on display. Old microchips, defunct websites from the 90's and not least of all: the Steve Jobs Pavilion, which I definitely would have ducked into, had James not been keeping such a serious clip.

As we rushed out of the terminal there was a white Mercedes Maybach parked at the curb—snow white, in and out. Cocaine seats, as Jay-Z would have said. He and Kanye were the only reasons I even knew what a Maybach was. It's a million dollar ride. Literally. We didn't have those in the Midwest.

"James, stop for a second." I was a couple yards behind and frantically pulling out my phone. "I want to get a picture." The ride probably belonged to a Saudi prince or Sean Parker. This was California—As Seen On TV. James, perhaps trying to impress me, didn't break stride. He stepped right up to it and pretended to open the trunk. I started laughing nervously, expecting a bum rush at any second. "Dude, that's funny, but let's not mess with that car." I put away my phone and started to look around nervously. "Do you know how much that thing costs?"

James looked slightly offended at my question. "1.4 million dollars," he answered, as the trunk popped open. "Mr. Graft bought a fleet of them so he got a bulk discount."

"What the hell..." And then the light broke through. "Are you saying this car...is for us?"

"Yes, sir," James said casually, loading the bags and shutting the trunk.

I swallowed awkwardly, and took a deep breath, inhaling the room temperature weather, and looking out over the complete precision of the California landscape.

The palm trees in the median stood sentinel over a perfectly manicured scene of sand, grass and sun. I looked down at the reflection of the sky in the hood of the car—the infinite blue washing over the chrome.

"Mr. Middle?" James asked. "Are you feeling all right?"

"Yes," I said, as if it were the answer to a quiz.

"There is water in the car, and if you need anything--something stronger, perhaps..." He gave a barely perceptible nod. "Just ask."

I climbed clumsily into the back seat, afraid to make contact with the snowflake leather. The wheels in my head turned, registering the implications of million dollar cars, never mind a staff to spit and polish them. What was I stepping into? I started picturing pet elephants, and a Chihuahua wearing the Hope Diamond.

Monogrammed bottles of water were chilling in the sink of the white polished oak bar in the back seat. I struggled to open one of them and drained it in one long gulp. Much better. I really didn't fathom how loaded this Graft guy was. I'd never actually met him. I mean, I knew Maisey's family had fuck-you money, but this wasn't just *fuck you*. This was fuck-you-and-your-mother-and-everyone-else money. This was the one percent of the one percent.

"Holy shit, James," I reflected, taking in the whole scene.

Our eyes met in the rearview mirror. "Not sure how holy it is."

We spun through cycles of freeway interchanges with its drivers holding their breath. Then we were looped out to the west and headed toward the redwood hills that separate Silicon Valley from the ocean. Everything smelled like sunshine and crisp new air. We pulled off the highway and passed the urban sprawl and tract houses, ugly in their quaint beauty. After a while the houses gave way to a vast unpopulated expanse.

"This is the wetlands," James explained as we drove through several miles of undeveloped marsh. "It's a protected area. Agave is on the other side of this stretch." It was a vast expanse of nothing, in either direction. No buildings, no houses. James slowed after a while and turned onto an unmarked road. There was a brick station house and we got a wink from a gate guard inside the window as a twelve-foot iron fence slowly opened.

I saw two signs just ahead: one for West Agave and one for East Agave.

"East and West?" I asked. "What's the difference?"

He shot me a glance in the rearview, as we took the East Agave turn. "The West is what some folks refer to as new-new money. And the East is the proper, old-new money."

I gave him a sideways look. "Well, either way you look, it all just looks like *too much* money," I joked.

He gave me another wordless glance via the rearview and drove the Maybach down a well-kept dirt road with unpaved sidewalks and perfectly manicured high hedges on either side. Every ½ mile or so there was an entrance to a house, and in the distance you could make out the roofs or the tips of a spire over the tall trees that barricaded the residences.

"Why the dirt roads?" I asked.

"East Agave had the paved roads removed last year for aesthetic reasons. Mr. Graft says it lends itself a certain authenticity." We made eye contact in the mirror. "Mrs. Graft doesn't quite like it. I believe she suggested marble instead."

"Marble roads?" I laughed. "How does anyone even get this much money?"

"Not sure I want to know, Mr. Middle."

We took a right down a driveway. Sculpted hedges, dotted with yellow roses for fifty yards or so. The lane broke open into a front yard that approached Versailles levels of grandeur. If Louis the XIV was a rap star from the South, this is where he'd live. A southern plantation on steroids. There was a twelve-car garage, a greenhouse the size of a gymnasium, massive gardens in all directions, stables and tennis courts. It just went on. I guess if you're gonna inhabit the most expensive real estate in North America you might as well go all the way.

I began to doubt I would even survive the week.

We turned off the main driveway and onto a path toward a small guesthouse done up in the same white, faux-colonial manner as the main house. A mini-McMansion with ivy creeping around the edges. James met my gaze in the rearview again.

"Dinner will be brought down for you around six o'clock if that's alright, Mr. Middle."

James set my bags down on the white carpet of the cottage's living room. Even this guest cottage seemed nicer than any house I'd ever been in. By like a hundred times.

"Mrs. Graft has selected your menu for each day she is gone," he continued.

Maisey and Reed were on the tail end of their whirlwind tour of Europe, bouncing from country to country like a gold-plated pinball. They travelled, I would learn, when the sedentary life that Agave afforded became too stale.

"The rich exercise by running from their problems," my father imparted to me on my sixteenth birthday. It was in response to an inquiry I made about our wealthier family counterparts who had moved to the East and West Coasts. I think he must have seen it in me then: the sparkle of ambition in my eyes.

"Will there be anything else, Mr. Middle?"

"Charlie, man." I corrected James yet again. "You can call me Charlie."

"I really can't, Mr. Middle. But thank you." He fixed me with a polite nod. "If you need a car you can use the paging system; there are directions on your nightstand."

I stared at him nervously then searched my pockets.

"No, Mr. Middle," he gestured with his hands as if I were about to pull a gun. "You do not tip the staff."

"Oh, okay... Sorry."

"It's not a problem," he turned a slight smile and there was an awkward silence. "...Mr. Charlie."

"That's almost worse, James," I laughed. "But it's the thought that counts."

By the time I had unpacked the very few items that I owned, I was feeling better. Who cares if I was outclassed? After all, I was here, wasn't I? I didn't have to forge birth records or lie about my income. I was invited. Then an unfettered optimism began to take over. I was on my own for the first time—the rest of my life squarely within my grasp. I felt invincible.

I decided to take a walk around the vast, perfectly unnatural lake that separated East and West Agave. Making my way along its western shore, a perfect blend of unspoiled natural radiance and golf-course-chic, I noticed most of the massive estates looked like they had no one living there. Not abandoned, just uninhabited.

The world felt so empty that I was startled when I spotted a lone figure dotting the perimeter of the water: a man, or boy, probably not much older than me, stood astride the postmodern architecture that lined the edges of his lawn. You could tell it was his lawn by the way he stood on it.

He didn't see me, or at least he didn't acknowledge me. So I just watched quietly from beside a weeping willow. He wasn't more than fifty feet away on a jetty that extended from his property, with an unmoving gaze toward the water. He stood like he had a purpose. Like the earth spun around him.

I wanted to be this guy from the moment I saw him. A lean figure cut by an able blade, in perfect harmony with the dusky shade of the falling sun.

He stretched his arms out toward the water, as if he were reaching across the lake to pull something toward him. Or maybe push something back.

```
enter=jss
// ----------------------------------------------
----------------------------
<p>This <em>is</em> a paragraph</p>
      <div id="content">
         <enter="<see .frame> dif=you>"
      <h1> The Title</h1>
      .frame=CAN
<p>Some content</p>
</br> "<find>" a> @frame
            </div>
            </body>
// ----------------------------------------------
----------------------------
```

"**D**ude, your momz is really cool with you staying out all night?" Anthony mumbled through a mouthful of burger.

Joss Stember was sitting across from Anthony, Eddy, Ciccu and Lenny at the original Tommy's in Canoga. It was the cusp of summer, 2009. The bright red tables and yellow umbrellas made it feel like a real birthday. Seventeen. Joss didn't know what seventeen meant. But he knew what Tommy's Burgers meant.

"Sort of," he answered.

"This was a damn good choice for your birthday lunch, kid," Lenny remarked, a dollop of ketchup dotting his crisp white t-shirt like a gunshot. He looked down, his slick black hair reflecting in the sunlight.

"Yeah, he'll be eating lobster and pig truffles tonight," Eddy drawled in a snooty voice. He had dark curly hair and a black smudge splashed across his left cheek.

"Pigs don't have truffles, you grease monkey. They find them," Lenny corrected.

They all looked at Lenny, eight eyebrows raised

"I saw it on this cooking show," he quickly countered. "My mom used to make me watch it..." he trailed off.

All five boys broke into a raucous laugh.

"Well," Eddy added, gesturing to Joss. "Our boy here'll be eatin' more than lobster if he's lucky." Another chorus of amusement echoed followed by some overzealous back patting, which Joss shrugged off.

"Yeah, I sure do like me some rich food," Ciccu added a little too late. Then, as if they hadn't got the joke, he held up two fingers and half-heartedly stuck his tongue between them. "You know *rich food.*"

"Yeah, we know, Ciccu," Lenny said, wearily. "We know your momma's bed came with a retaining wall."

The 250-pound Ciccu got halfway out of his seat like he was ready to throw down. His size got the best of him, though, and he came crashing down on his seat with a thud that rattled the trays of food off the table. The guys laughed so hard Eddy coughed up an onion. Ciccu lowered his head and started picking at his chili fries.

"Guys," Anthony reprimanded. "This is a special occasion. Let's keep it classy." He stood up, raising his Mountain Dew and tapped it with a biodegradable Spork. "To our homey, Joss: May your seventeenth year bring you all the more closer to your dreams." Eyes rolled at the table and Lenny threw some fries in Anthony's direction. But he continued unperturbed, "And may your dreams involve getting sand in places that you didn't know you had, with girls that you never thought you could get."

A raucous cheer erupted but died quickly as the manager approached.

$$$

"How are your folks, man?" Anthony asked Joss after they broke from the rest of the pack. "Are you having a family party before you go out tonight?" They were walking down Victory Boulevard, toward Joss' street. Anthony was wearing a button-up shirt tucked into old school Levi's and a pair of black Converse. He always looked crisp, Joss thought to himself, like he was going to church. His black hair slicked back, and the sides neatly shaved.

"They're good." Joss responded. "We had donuts this morning. They're both doing a lot of overtime lately; money's all right but I never see them."

"I heard Jake got his scholarship to CAL. They should be proud. You guys—that's what they're doing it for." Anthony was always far more of an adult than Joss could ever imagine himself being. He had to be. After his dad went AWOL a few years back, Anthony had been saddled with taking care of his mother and grandma.

"Oh, they definitely are," Joss answered, a bit more defensively than he intended. "I mean, we're all proud," he corrected himself.

Anthony looked at him for longer than was comfortable. They walked silently for a block or so. The old oaks on these streets were overgrown as if trying to hide the weathered homes that lined the rusty block. Joss knew enough not to ask about Anthony's family, lest it remind Anthony of the impending deluge he was barely holding back.

"Don't let any of those rich Malibu girls break your heart now. You're a Reseda boy." Anthony started shadow boxing. "Remember what side of the tracks you're from. Represent." He gave Joss a playful shove. It was almost as if Anthony forced himself, in these moments, to squeeze out any remaining grit from the tube of childhood.

"Rich girls breaking my heart?" Joss smiled back at Anthony. "I should be so lucky."

Anthony tipped an invisible hat to Joss as they parted ways. "I'll see you, homey," Anthony called back as he crossed the street. "Text me updates."

Joss took a shortcut through the alleyway, war-torn with sagging fences, burnt lawns and barely-leashed dogs. Halfway down he hopped over a brick wall with healthy vines pouring over its edges and landed in his backyard. It was well kept--in direct contrast to the neighborhood's concrete jungle motif. He wondered when his mom found the time. He never saw her out here. He never saw her at all, lately. The power-saw from the guy across the street was almost in time with the bass bump and rattle of his next-door neighbor's monster truck. If any of his family were ever home long enough they might complain about the constant barrage of sound. But as it was, they barely noticed it. He didn't have to call out to see if anyone was home; he knew they weren't. His Dad, a plumbing supervisor for the city, was at another night shift. His mom, a nurse, the same. Joss knew exactly who they were working for. Just like Anthony said. And he kept his shit straight because of it.

But Joss didn't have any freakish natural ability to pound people into the grass of a football field like his brother did, so he would have to cure cancer or solve world hunger to get any chance at a scholarship to Cal or Stanford. Or even UCLA. He and his parents researched minority scholarships but you basically have to be an endangered species to have ethnicity matter anymore.

Maybe Joss didn't play sports like his brother, but that doesn't mean he was unmotivated. Lumbering up to his room, its décor comprised of parachute window shades, obscure posters of bands most people hadn't heard of, and an empty aquarium, he was already thinking about the program. He flipped open his laptop, a homemade special, and leaned back contemplating the screen. He breathed deeply and then typed: remake.exe. Several boxes blossomed open and cascaded across the screen. Each one with a video still.

All of the time his brother would've spent running laps and tossing a friggin' ball around Joss channeled into computers. Programming. Joss was a hacker, though among the group of online friends who he shared his crude programs with, that term was not allowed. He wasn't half bad, either. And what he may have lacked in skill he made up for in creativity. His pals in the online consortium didn't have enough time or money to spend on anything meaningful--stupid games, crap to keep them stimulated and entertained. It wasn't like they tried very hard.

Until *remake.exe*.

He didn't want to admit it, but Joss had become mildly obsessed with the program. It had started with him trying to find the best way to take a video of Geezer, one of his hacker friends, and then get Geezer's lips to mouth the words of a clip from Twilight, his least favorite movie. Putting the audio in was no problem, but making the lips work well was a pain in the ass. It was originally just supposed to be a quick practical joke. But as Joss was assembling the code he saw that he could theoretically reverse the process and put Geezer into the Twilight clip and make it look real: have Geezer's actual face morph onto Edward Cullen's alabaster skin. That may sound simple, but it's actually hard to be simple when it comes to code. Joss was not a genius hacker but this *was* a genius piece.

16

His older brother Jake swung in through Joss' doorway via the barely used chin-up bar. Joss startled from the sea of ones and zeroes and squinted his eyes in pain.

"Dude," Jake said in disgust, "you're not even ready?" Jake tossed a pair of black jeans and a red leather jacket on the bed. "There ya go, birthday boy. Don't say I never did anything for you."

Joss surveyed the wardrobe his brother had picked out. "I'm gonna look like the Karate Kid."

"Just wear it," Jake said impatiently, swinging back down the hall. "The eighties are your friend."

Joss looked out his window. The sun had gone down. He checked the clock on the computer: 7:30. "Holy crap," he said, steadying himself. He'd really gotten sucked in. He rubbed his blurred-out eyes. How did I lose six hours, he thought, saving his work and shutting the laptop. He stood up, almost losing his balance, eyed Jake's clothes suspiciously. "I'm gonna get my ass kicked in this."

$$$

"Jossy," Jake warned as they sped up Victory Boulevard, top-down, in Jake's flat black CJ7 Jeep from god knows what year. "Even though it's your birthday, you know you're gonna have to let Santander sit shotgun."

"Whatever," Joss shouted against the wind and blasting music. "Just don't call me Jossy again."

Jake laughed then glanced to his left, where some girl in another car was waving at him. Her lane stopped and theirs rolled forward; Jake waved goodbye as they sped away. "Two cars passing in the night," Joss remarked, wondering where his share of the glorious DNA that Jake had stocked up on. It was all so easy for him.

Jake wooted a few times then bellowed: "We're gonna show you how the one percent live tonight, baby brother." The gas stations and taquerias and liquor stores flashed by on either side of Victory Boulevard like runway lights. They were taxiing, preparing to take off out of the gritty San Fernando Valley and fly over the sparkly canyons, landing in the Disneyland of high school parties. They picked up Santander in a twenty-second slowdown, and made their ascent through the canyon, past houses that looked like they were hanging on for dear life. "How does anyone live there?" Joss remembered wondering as a kid. He still wondered.

The city of Malibu is more or less a fictional place, even though it's real. It exists inside a bubble separated from the golden triangle of Hollywood, LA and the San Fernando Valley, populated by a lot of movie and TV execs and some A-list actors. It's almost as if it really is a back lot of some studio where the cameras are always rolling—the place where the rich play out there own version of reality TV. But it's closed-circuit TV, not for the public. You can't spend too much time there if you're not one of the fortunate ones. "Someone's always watching," Joss had once told Anthony. "To ensure continuity. And if you hang around too long they find a way to kick you out."

As the three of them headed out the canyon and into the town, a twenty-foot burst of flame shot up from the side of the mountain, fifty feet ahead. It came out of a long cylinder jutting upwards toward the sky, nestled in the hillside near where the canyon road begins to descend into the town center of Malibu. It was a place called Rockedyne where they build jets and turbine engines. Joss took a field trip there in fifth grade. Whenever he'd pass it and see the flames shoot up he considered it good luck.

A few minutes later Jake took a hard right onto Pacific Coast Highway. They headed north, away from the center of town, toward a stretch of supersized McMansions clustered together on the beach. They were like a group of football players on steroids bullying the smaller houses around them. And then they were there: Point Dume. Santander said that it was Brogan Landing's house, the billionaire media mogul. Mr. Landing, Joss presumed, would not be in attendance.

Brogan's son Proctor was a senior and the one having the soiree. Normally, Joss wouldn't even have heard of this party, let alone thought about going. But Jake, being the football celebrity that he was, basically got treated like a rock star in the high school party circuit. It gave him a free pass through the socio-economic border checks that were there to keep the rest of the unwashed masses out. Part of Jake couldn't give a shit about it all, but there was another part that envied his brother's access.

"Should we go by net worth tonight, or by the hotness index?" Santander asked Jake, who only grinned.

"Both," Jake answered Santander. "Bonus points if their boyfriends are actually at the party."

The gates to the Point Dume neighborhood opened and the CJ7 rolled on through. "What about you, little man," Santander asked, turning around to take inventory of Joss. "You finally gonna carve a notch on that empty belt?"

Joss had, if it was possible, negative cred. While he was sure Jake had enough to lend him for the night, he feared the elite partygoers would be able to smell mediocrity. And it wouldn't take long for them to locate its source. As they entered, Joss noticed Jake and Santander glide in like royalty. Heads of hot girls leaned toward each other, whispers and smiles, tongues on lips.

Their eyes moved past Jake and Santander, searching expectantly for the rest of their entourage, and fell with a dull thud on Joss. It was a visible let down and the grazing herd quickly averted their gaze as if to not infect themselves. To his credit, Jake tried to make Joss feel a part of it between intervals of flirting and taking beer bongs. But there was only so much he could do; it was in Joss' hands. And Joss' hands were in his pockets.

So Joss retreated, looking for potential sanctuary from the crowd until it was time to go. The house was big enough to get lost in, but that didn't help Joss. Every room he ended up in eventually got taken over by kids looking for a discreet place to get high or get it on. At one point he ended up in a room that was actually an aquarium—all four walls made of clear Plexiglas with exotic fish that swum around like UFOs in orbit. At first he felt like he'd entered an alien civilization, where he was on display—all the fish and bizarre sea creatures staring at him. Then it occurred to him that the creatures on the other side of the glass were actually less alien to him than the partygoers on the other side of the door. After all, there was no pretense to being a fish, exotic or not: you just swam, fed and shit. Humans made the simplest things so complicated.

Deciding to avoid the house altogether, Joss made his way down to the beach, which was also littered with partygoers. Girls running drunk and naked into the ocean, egged on by the catcalls from their sodded peers. Games of touch football where the girl running with the ball would inevitably get tackled and end up at the bottom of a pile of sweaty boys. The typical teenage bacchanalia you'd expect from a Malibu party. There was a bonfire that a couple dozen kids were dancing around, singing something unfamiliar, maybe a collegiate fight song that their parents or older siblings had taught them. It reminded Joss of a film he saw in AP History about the youth movements of Berlin in the 1930's.

He had to walk down the beach a bit before he found an unpopulated hideaway, between a cluster of high rocks that formed a u-shape, opening up toward the ocean. When he settled inside the rocky shelter, the clamor from down the beach melted away. He eased down into the velvety Malibu sand. His phone buzzed for the ten-thousandth time. It was Anthony messaging to see how it was going:

"Hope you're doing things that you'll be ashamed of in the morning! You deserve it, homey."

Joss turned his phone off and looked up at a sky swelling with stars. You don't get a view like this in the San Fernando Valley, he thought. All the stars hide over there. I guess it's only in Malibu or Montana that they feel safe enough to come out. "I don't blame them," he murmured.

"Too much to drink or too much to smoke," a voice startled him from somewhere up on the rocks.

"Neither," he answered, cursing the fact that he couldn't seem to get away, and not caring at that point about putting up a pretext. "Just nowhere to hide."

"Ahh," the girl's voice cooed. "Right answer."

Joss could hear her move down from the high rock she must have been perched on then drop with a tiny thud onto the sand behind him. He didn't move. He was too exhausted at that point to care what anyone thought. He just wanted to go home.

"It's like the Hitler Youth meets Beach Blanket Bingo over there," the girl deadpanned as she came up behind him and plopped herself down on the sand.

Joss tore his gaze away from the starry night trying to get a look at her. "That's... exactly what I was thinking," he said, taken aback, letting out a breathy laugh.

He looked back to get a glimpse of her but she wasn't close enough to make out in the dark. "I take it you're not in their ranks?" Joss asked.

"It's complicated." She paused. "I guess you could say I was born behind enemy lines."

"Aha," Joss replied.

"Don't aha me," she said playfully. "It's not my fault. I didn't have a choice."

"Who does?"

"I'm Maisey," she extended her hand over Joss' chest and he gave an awkward shake.

"Joss."

"Sounds like both our parents had some issues to work out," she quipped.

"Yeah, well, at least I wasn't named Chad or Skip."

"Well their first choice for me was Ashley, so I consider myself lucky."

"Wow, you really did dodge a bullet with that one."

"Thanks, Jocelyn."

"Girl, I'm from Reseda. You're gonna have to do a lot better if you want to even scratch the surface of effective dissing."

"I'm sure once I hit the surface there wouldn't be much left to scratch."

"Touche, Malibu Barbie."

Maisey gave a playful kick to Joss' side, which inadvertently sprayed his face with sand. He jolted up reflexively, spitting out and blindly rubbing at his eyes.

"Oh my god, I'm sorry," Maisey apologized. She gently grabbed his hands and pulled them away from his eyes. "Don't rub, it makes it worse. You have to look down and blink."

Joss resisted stubbornly and then lowered his hands and blinked. It worked and he looked up at her face, hovering inches from his. He could finally see her. Cheekbones gliding into lips, chestnut eyes as big as anything he'd ever seen.

"Wait," she said softly. "Close your eyes again. You still have some sand on your eyelashes." Joss' eyes closed and Maisey's sweet breath blew against his face. His skin rippled, the blond hairs on his arms standing at attention like an orchestra tuning itself before the symphony begins. "I'm somewhat of a klutz, I guess," she said, looking at him with eyes so big he felt as if he were being swallowed.

He blinked again. Blood rushed—pulses of slow, wet current— and everything seemed to float as if gravity forgot what it was. A second, more irresistible wave of warmth passed through him as her hand cradled his cheek and her soft fingers made contact with his skin. There was an inch of breath between their lips; Joss could feel it more than see it.

And without any warning there was no distance at all, just the most tender parts of each of their bodies pressed together as if they had never been apart. There was no clawing or tearing at each other like you see in the movies. They were swimming in warm water, without needing to breathe. Effortless. Without thought or warning and without hesitation, the rest of their bodies pressed together, remembering for the first time what they were meant to do. Limbs slowly winding around each other like vines. Clothes dissolving, skin pressing together like the pages of a book, bound by a common spine. One long sentence, filled with the perfect words to tell the story of how it all happened. Commas that pulled the words apart and then back together again, without stopping the flow or hiding what they really meant.

It was impossible to tell when they actually fell asleep because they started dreaming when they were still awake. Joss remembered watching the colors of the sky appear across Maisey's naked midriff: the explosion of violet, the crashing of orange and the promise of yellow.

"Will you marry me," he asked her, half-asleep.

"Someday," she whispered.

CHAPTER THREE

There was a rumbling followed by shouts and what sounded like a tornado warning. I was nestled in my post-colonial cocoon far from the front drive of the Graft house, but I startled into consciousness as if the racket were coming from outside my bedroom door. I got dressed and rushed up the bank through a thicket of bushes and into the front yard of the main house. There was a line of a half dozen cars parked in the drive with people in various stages of entering the abode. Music blared from several of the cars and created a grayed-out sonic landscape. I approached warily, across the vast lawn, and crept up the steps, hesitating at the last second. Was it a mistake to barge in? What is the protocol here? I should just go back, I decided.

As I turned to bail, the front door opened. James was there. He gave me a nod and stared at my pants. I looked down to see my zipper undone. "Uhh... Thanks," I said to him, repairing the breach and stepping into the grand foyer.

"Of course, sir," he said, with the slightest hint of a smile.

"Is that Charlie Middle, pure as the Midwest snow, blown into my house?"

It was a voice as sweet as it was loud, and I knew it immediately. I just stood in the blinding white entryway, disoriented. The marble floor was veined in gold with twin grand staircases spiraling up like Cartier Dragons and a chandelier the size of a house hanging precariously from a sixty-foot ceiling. Behind my approaching cousin I noticed a crowd of people being ushered in through the other side of the entryway.

"Oh we rushed as fast as we could to get back to you!" Maisey threw her arms around me and I let out an involuntary belly laugh. She's the type of girl who could force you into an involuntary belly laugh and a senseless smile. Magnificence like hers is reserved for private collections, not museums. They don't let the public near that kind of beauty.

"I didn't think you'd remember me," I said, lips pressed against teeth. The temperature in the room shot up as she took hold of me and I had to remind myself that she was family.

Her arms were locked around me and her face was buried in my chest. "Bring me back to the Midwest, Charlie. This instant. Make me pure again!"

A well-built man with tan arms, white pants and a pink polo shirt seemed to glide across the polished stone floor. "I don't think the good people of the Midwest would know what to do with you," he jibed.

Maisey shot him a resentful glance.

"Reed Graft," the pink-shirted man said to me, extending a tanned, well-muscled forearm. He had a watch that looked like it must have cost as much as a yacht. "A pleasure to meet you, Charlie. Maisey thinks the world of you."

"Really? I seriously didn't think she'd remember me. We haven't seen each other since my family visited LA when I was eight and she was, what, twelve? I remember her throwing a bunch of sand at me and then some crying."

"Well, she hasn't stopped talking about you the whole way home," Reed added.

"Dreadful," Maisey stared down and heaved a desperate sigh. "Dreadful, dreadful, dreadful!"

"What is it now," Reed asked with a comical roll of his eyes, as if this were all rehearsed.

"I have a pebble in my shoe," she twisted her ankle back and forth until her shoe slipped off. It was strangely erotic somehow. I caught myself staring at her for a second too long and looked up. Reed met my eyes with a knowing wink and I looked away, trying to brush it off. "Reed, can't you do something about these abominable roads. Why do these people insist on this madness?" She stared back up at me. "Does it make sense to you, Charlie Middle? That one would tear up a perfectly good road?"

She decided to take her other shoe off and rubbed her feet together.

"The whims of fools, the whims of fools." She looked lost for a second captured by a far off place then snapped back. "Next thing you know we'll be living in huts, foraging for berries…" She seemed to ponder that. "It doesn't sound that bad, really. Do you forage for things back in the Midwest, Charlie Middle? Please tell me you do."

"Only when Taco Bell is closed," I answered.

We all laughed harder than we should have. "You are a gem, a complete and utter gem." Maisey brought her hand to my cheek and cradled it as if I were a porcelain doll.

"As long as they accept credit cards, I imagine Maisey would handle the wild just fine," Reed jested.

James approached Reed. "There's a call for you, sir."

A microscopic look passed between Maisey and Reed. "Excuse me, Charlie," Reed nodded.

"It must be an *emergency*," Maisey said, "for someone to be calling at such an hour." The words seemed to chase Reed as he hustled out of the entryway. Maisey took a deep breath, and then turned back to me with her bubbly charm intact. "You are an absolute sight for sore eyes, Charlie Middle," she gushed, taking my arm and leading us into the deeper recesses of the house. "You will run away with me, won't you?"

"As fast as I can," I smiled at her.

We sat down in a gold-plated room with a fire blazing--even though it was probably eighty degrees outside. Some of the guests were sitting on a couch by the fire as if they were nursing frostbite.

"That's quite a fire," I commented.

"Is it too hot, would you like me to turn on the air conditioning?" she asked without irony.

"No," I said, biting back a snide comment. "I'm fine."

"What do you think of our humble home? Is it just atrocious and appalling?"

"Are you kidding? It's the most unbelievable thing I've ever seen," I lied. "Thank you so much for—"

"Stop." She put her fingers to my lips. "Stop this instant. You are forbidden-- *forbidden*, Charlie Middle--to do anything but accept the things that are given to you as if you deserved them all."

"I'll try," I promised, holding her hand.

"Herve," Maisey said to one of the guests sitting by the fire. "Meet my absolutely wonderful cousin, Charlie Middle."

Herve, I observed, had his right hand buried in between the thighs of his companion. He removed his hand with a slight look of contempt and extended it to me. *Ewww*, I thought, but took it nonetheless and shook. "Se vas." He muttered and then went back to business.

Maisey laughed off his brusqueness. "Herve is a count and comes from one of the oldest and richest families in Europe. He's thinking about buying Facebook, now that the shares are almost worthless."

Reed came back in and took a seat on one of the gilded chairs. "Hmm," she grumbled, looking reproachfully away from him.

"Couldn't be helped," he remarked and took a hit off his vodka tonic. Reed's blue eyes swam and his brown hair dangled above his brow. "I see Herve has already begun his due diligence," he quipped trying to change the subject. He looked like an ad for Remy Martin or something. It was all too perfect, like he'd been practicing sitting in that chair his whole life. And, in a way, I guess he had.

"Where is Mark," Maisey inquired still a little salty. "I thought he and Herve were supposed to be socializing."

"Mark Zuckerberg is here?" I asked with all the tact of a fanboy.

"Mark is, uhh… indisposed at the moment," Reed answered Maisey, a mischievous glint in his eye. "Let's just say he's changed his status from public to private."

The phone rang again and you could see Reed's eyes dart nervously toward Maisey. Her eyes slit and you could see a pain disguised as rage start to surface. The tension immediately ratcheted up to ten.

"It's getting late and I'm sure we're all more tired than we realize." Reed sounded like he was bargaining.

"There's a lot more to everything than we realize." Maisey clutched her martini glass and jabbed at an olive with a tiny red sword.

"Perhaps I should get back to bed," I said getting up.

"Nonsense," Maisey demanded, keeping her gaze fixed on Reed while placing her arm on my shoulder. "Reed can go play with his friends, while you tell me absolutely everything about absolutely everything."

"Let the poor boy go to bed," Reed said impatiently.

A thick silence settled heavily, and I was grateful when James entered the room again. He stopped at the top of the stairs and nodded at Reed.

"Couldn't be helped," Maisey said, her voice cracking slightly. She looked at me, tears welling in her eyes and pulled herself into my chest. "I'm sorry, Charlie," she sniffed. I *will* see you in the morning..."

She let go and turned away from Reed as she fled. I could hear her footsteps break into a run and a distant "Couldn't be helped!" echoed from a far-off place.

"Sorry about that, Old Sport," Reed said to me with an expensive grin. "Jet lag, you know... Probably best we let you get back to bed."

"Yes," I said, eyeing the hallway Maisey had escaped to. "But are you sure I shouldn't..."

"I can handle putting her to bed. And if I can't one of her girls will."

I took a deep breath and pulled myself up to a standing position. I felt hot all of a sudden and unsure about the world. James nodded and offered to drive me down to the guesthouse.

"I think I can make it on my own," I assured him.

"I don't mind," he pressed.

"I do," I nearly snapped back at him.

We both looked at each other, and he nodded once more. There was something in his eyes that told me he was as revolted as I was by this whole scene. But it was tucked away in a safe place. Over the course of the summer, I would learn to do the same.

```
// --------------------------------------------------
----------------------------
<html>strong<em0>is</em0>enough</p>
    strong <head>="content">
    strong <body>"type"
      < ladyaofd.thx"e a=can></y=9on>"
      <h1>Everything</h1>
        <p>always</p>
<breaks>a=<part>

// --------------------------------------------------
----------------------------
```

A '65 mustang, red with a black top. Maisey could have had any car in the world for her sixteenth birthday, and that's what she chose.

It was better than perfect. Not that Joss needed anything else on which to base his instant and absolute love for her. The top was down and the late morning sun felt like a bath. Joss had woken up a new person, whole somehow where he had been in parts. But everything had come together that morning. Maisey, sitting next to him, her white linen dress waving in the wind like a flag of surrender. His own surrender. She had aviators on and her copper-blond hair was pulled back loosely; she glanced over at him with a smile that made Joss want to start a religion.

Her eyes returned to the road. The canyon's no place to screw around. There are handmade wreaths of freshly picked flowers dotting the road along the corridor, tied with ribbons that show the names of the people who went over. At the bend of a steep curve, halfway through, there's a huge memorial to a CHP officer. A badge made out of mosaic tile. It always sobered Joss to think that if a cop who did this for a living can go off, he certainly could.

"The memorials always trip me out," Maisey said, both hands on the top of the walnut steering wheel. "Do you know anyone who's gone over?"

"No." Joss answered. "My brother has a friend who knew a guy from Grant who did."

"Was it an accident?"

"They reported it as one, I guess."

"Cause a lot of them aren't," she said.

Joss looked at her with a concerned gaze.

Maisey laughed, "I'm sorry, I'm not trying to be morbid. It just makes me think, you know."

"Yes," he said soberly. "I know." Joss put his hand on her leg.

"I know this is weird," she glanced nervously at Joss. "But remember when I said I didn't want you to worry about being with anyone; that it would be fine with me?"

"Yes," Joss laughed as if it were a joke.

"Well if you *didn't* want to, you know, be with anyone else. I wouldn't want that statement I made to make you feel you should, necessarily." She put her hand on Joss' leg and everything stood at attention. "I mean it's whatever you want. That's what I'm trying to say."

"It's hilarious that you think this is even an issue," Joss looked at her with an amused smile.

"You'll see. Once a girl's into you, other girls pick up on it." She nodded, keeping her eyes on the road. "It's a scent."

"I'll start wearing body spray," Joss joked.

"Ugh," she scrunched her face. "Maybe this isn't gonna work out."

They laughed and held their breath as they went through a long tunnel, each of them making the same wish.

$$$

"It's unbelievable," Joss typed.

"It hasn't even been thirty seconds yet," Maisey typed back.

"I know; that's how good it is."

It was six weeks later. Joss was lying on his bedroom floor, legs draped up over the side of his bed, his laptop sitting on his chest. He was wearing his bigger, nicer earphones, the 99Xs that his parents got him for his last birthday.

"Mmmm," Joss let out a delighted moan.

He was listening to a song Maisey had recorded and sent over. She had one of those smoky voices, but bright, and light as a feather somehow. The way she sang, it was like she was just talking to him. And the guitar--sparse, hollow like the night air, an invisible clothesline to hang her words on. It was so beautiful he couldn't even believe he knew the person who made it, let alone that it was made for him.

"Every hair on my body is standing straight up right now," Joss typed.

"I wish I could see that **," Maisey typed back.

"Beeeeehaaaave!"

"I love you."

"I'm almost done then we can go back to video," Joss typed. "Oh… and I love you too."

"By the way," Maisey continued. "I broke my phone today and couldn't get a new one. So I won't be able to text until we arrive in Paris tomorrow night.

"That sucks. ☹"

"Major. Oh, and I have a doctor's appointment tomorrow; my dad's taking me before we leave. I'm sure it's nothing. Some bug."

"Have you told him about us yet?"

"The doctor?"

"Haha."

"Not yet," Maisey typed back. "But I think he already knows."

"What?"

"I know he already knows"

"What?!"

"He knows everything, Joss. He's the head of a friggin' media empire. Bringing it up can wait a few more weeks til I'm there to physically defend you."

Joss stopped typing.

"Joke!" Maisey typed.

"Is it even slightly odd that we're texting each other," Maisey typed. "When we could be on vid?"

"Weird is an underrated concept."

"☹"

"Switching to vidchat now. Over and out."

$$$

The next evening came and Joss had still not heard from Maisey. He'd gone back and reread their texts. Strange, he thought. She said she'd call or IM. He began to itch in withdrawal, waiting for her to come online. 8:30. Nothing. 10:15. Nothing. 11:45. Nothing.

Was she alright? She wouldn't *not* contact him. They hadn't missed a day of electronic communication in the last six weeks. Maybe there's no connection where she is. Maybe she didn't want to use her dad's cell, or she couldn't get away from him long enough to call. It could be no big deal. *It is no big deal,* he tried to convince himself.

12:28. Nothing. 1:55.

Joss called every Paris hotel he could find online that had four or five stars. Nothing.

He woke up drooling in the exact position he was the night before—back on the floor, legs up on the bed, laptop on his chest. The sun snuck in through a rip in the curtain and struck Joss directly in the eye. He registered the laptop on his chest and swiped the track pad to take it off sleep.

9:45. Nothing.

That's it, Joss said to himself. He had no choice and probably waited longer than he should have. There was no alternative than to go to the Landing house and try to find out something from them. Was he being ridiculous? It was a little extreme, he reflected, but these are extreme times. Her father's with her anyway, so it'll just be the maid or something. But he was still likely to find more info there than he had online. Joss had been data mining Google, setting up news alerts, searching for plane, train or automobile accidents—any kind of accidents, any news involving Maisey or Brogan Landing. That's the kind of thing that would have a billion hits. But there'd been nothing.

Both his parents had taken their cars. And his brother was up in Berkeley for a football orientation. The bus it was. All the way to Malibu, which took about eight transfers. There was no bus line to take him the rest of the distance North on PCH so he had to walk for a couple miles. When he finally arrived at the gate, Joss was even less composed than he was before. He was sweaty and nervous and aware that he probably should have dressed better. He worried they might think he was a stalker or a nutball and call the police.

Composing himself, he reached his hand up to the buzzer. Before he could even push the call button the gate began to open. Joss walked through, tentatively making his way up the cobblestone driveway to the elephantine doors that stood like menacing sentries. They too opened before he could even ring the bell.

A middle-aged man in a navy blazer stood at the doorway and nodded his head. "Good day, sir. Mr. Landing is expecting you."

"Mr. Landing," Joss asked, confused. "Isn't he in Europe?"

"Mr. Landing arrived back this morning," the man offered.

For some reason Joss hadn't registered how high profile Mr. Landing actually was. As he was led down the hall to his office, he couldn't help but take in the memorabilia from so many movies and TV shows. Awards pinned to the wall and a sea of faces looking out of 5x10 frames: Steve Jobs, Bill Clinton, Jay-Z, Jimmy Iovine, the Dalai Lama, Brad and Angelina, Vladimir Putin. And the one common denominator in all the photos was Mr. Landing's crooked smile, the one he was giving Joss from across the massive desk. "Why don't you have a seat closer to me, son." His hand waved and Joss' body reacted, almost as if it were connected to Landing's fat fingers. They shook hands over the desk, without Landing actually getting up.

Joss guzzled down a bottle of water that was offered to him.

"Did you walk here?" Landing half-joked. He was wearing a pink sweater with yellow shirt collars sticking out the neck. His face was a reddish brown that can only be achieved through years of heavy exposure and drinking.

"Part of the way," Joss answered, before he realized Landing was being sarcastic.

"Well," Landing gave an awkward glance. "I already know why you are here, Joss." He tilted his head in a way that could have taken as sympathy or perhaps resignation.

Joss involuntarily leaned toward the desk, "Is she all right?" He had a sinking feeling all of a sudden, as if he knew the next words that were about to come out. He could see it in Landing's eyes. Something was definitely wrong.

"She's going to be all right," Landing assured him, maintaining a cautious expression. "With some rest and care."

Joss' entire body unclenched, and he exhaled.

"However, and I am truly sorry for this, Maisey has chosen to cut off contact with you. For the foreseeable future," Landing added matter-of-factly.

38

The words took the air out of Joss's lungs. Out of the room.

"She's graduating early and then spending the summer as an intern at one of our magazines." Mr. Landing paused taking a deep, ponderous sigh. "She's not coming home, Joss."

"I don't understand, " Joss raised his hand in confusion. "Are you telling me you don't want me to see your daughter?"

"No, Joss." Landing shook his head and closed his eyes. "I'm saying *my daughter* does not want to see *you*."

Joss was ripped out of his reverie. "I don't... We've talked to each other every day for the last six weeks...She would have told me herself if she didn't want to see me. This is ridiculous..."

"Joss, I'm not the enemy here," Landing assured him, raising his palms up in defense.

"Who is?" Joss pleaded.

"Mother Nature," Landing sighed and looked down at his manicured hands. "Joss, this is more than I was supposed to share." He hesitated, glanced at Joss and then pressed on. "Maisey had an appointment at the doctor's before we left. Son... She was pregnant." The news fell on Joss' chest with a thud, burying him deep in his low-slung chair.

It felt true. He knew it was.

"The procedure went fine, no complications. But Maisey was..." Landing glanced out the window, trying to find the words. "...Inconsolable."

"You have to let me call her," Joss pleaded. "Please."

Landing tilted his head in a sympathetic gesture. "I know it's not completely your fault, Joss. And someday, perhaps with time, Maisey will realize the same. But right now, frankly, you are the last person in the world she wants to see."

Joss shook his head. "No. That can't be true."

"Son, you remind me of myself. A hard worker. With parents doing everything they can to get you a better life. You keep your nose clean, I see that. But I'm her father, Joss. And I'm afraid that takes precedence." He planted his hands firmly on the desk. "She has made herself abundantly clear and there is nothing I can do to alter that." Landing let out a sigh and looked at Joss. "I'll say one thing, though: time is the great healer."

Joss' brain was racing to keep up. He sat there, feeling his heart was melting off his sleeve.

"My suggestion is that you take time to process." Mr. Landing slid a slip of paper across the table. "I know this may seem awkward but I would like you to take this. I know how hard your family works." He paused. "But there's only so much they can do."

Joss picked up the slip of paper in a confused daze and had to look at it for several seconds before he registered what it was. He looked at the check in disbelief, and then at Landing. It was made to him, for one hundred thousand dollars.

"I'm not telling you what to do with the money," Landing assured Joss. "But certainly someone of your aptitude could use it as the basis for a top-notch education. Mr. Higgins mentioned you hadn't even considered applying to any four-year universities, due to funding issues."

Mr Higgins? Joss thought, completely bewildered. "My school counselor?" He had to catch his breath. "How do you know Mr. Higgins?"

40

"A man sits in that chair, Joss," Landing lifted his cigar and fixed Joss with a vice-grip stare. "I know more about him in the first five minutes, than he'll know about himself his whole life."

Joss tried to break free of Landing's paralyzing gaze. "I just want to see her one more time. Please."

"Joss," his eyes darkened slightly. "Put distance between this unfortunate turn of events. Let something good come of the pain." Landing gestured around his office at the accolades and awards. "I've built an empire out of trying to distract myself from my pain, from my loss."

Joss pushed back the check. "I'm sorry, sir. I don't want your money." He barely got out the words. "I don't want to be bought off. I want to see Maisey."

Landing gave a complicit nod. "I'm sorry if that's how this looks, son. That was not my intention." He took a deep breath. "Joss, there are moments when life takes turns. The right and wrong turns." He steadied his bejeweled hands on the desk and leaned in. "Joss, I just don't want to see someone with the potential that you have… get taken down by this. Not if I have the ability to help in some way."

"But…" is the only word Joss could come up with.

"Give it away if you want, the money is already set up in an account with your name." He studied Joss. "But don't think that this is anything less than a sincere gesture on my part, to extend my help in a difficult situation."

Landing leaned back again as to give him the floor, but Joss couldn't get a word out to save his life. So Landing filled the silence.

"I haven't arrived at where I am by giving away money, or making bad investments. I see you as a star Joss, and I want to make sure you're shooting up, not falling down."

A falling star and a shooting star are the same thing, Joss thought to himself, as every last bit of fight escaped him.

CHAPTER FIVE

I heard the music begin to play as I was reading a Retroverse programming manual, which had about the same effect as a napkin soaked in chloroform. I had sequestered myself in the guest cottage for some time alone. Maisey had kept me up most of the last week, with her infinite stories about foreign places and dignitaries and celebrities. She's basically met them all.

"Well, they all change so quick," she said. "One day they're there and the next they're gone. It's like everyone's involved in some dreadful illusion: people keep disappearing and the next thing you know new ones pop up."

Either way, the girl's got quite a rolodex. We had been to parties with all kinds of celebrities and billionaires. She even tried to set me up with some troubled teenage daughter of a senator. At first there was a bit of a spark. But after I had to help the poor girl vomit up some pills, my desire sort of shriveled up.

But tonight I was taking a much-needed hiatus from the attention, holed up in my bungalow trying to get back into the solitary groove from before the Grafts arrived back in town. At first I dismissed the mystery music as Maisey and Reed having friends over. Then it occurred to me that Maisey would have forced me to attend had she decided to throw a party. And the bump of the bass was coming from the other direction, across the water maybe. I took a deep breath and continued on with the Retroverse employee administration guidelines until my curiosity finally won out and I decided to go explore the source.

I made my way out of the cottage and down to the water line. Across the lake, there were lights and lasers spinning around like some carnival on acid. The music boomed across the water. So much so that I could almost make out the ripples moving in time to the beat as they made their way to the shore. It must have been a mile across but the crackle of voices and shrill laughter felt close enough that I could join in. It was all coming from the house where I had seen that guy standing the other day, looking out over the water.

I started to walk over but by the time I made it halfway around the lake, I chickened out. Sweats and a t-shirt probably wasn't appropriate attire for the festivities. Still, I wondered what the occasion was. Not that there seemed a need for an occasion with these people. Every night was like a Saturday and every Saturday like New Year's. I slunk back to my guesthouse feeling a little dejected. I could taste the party from here, and it felt free and electric. I tucked myself in and hoped it wouldn't be the last opportunity I had to visit the house.

The next morning an invitation arrived: brunch at the Graft's back patio. I had never had brunch at 3:00 in the afternoon, but I didn't remark on it. West coast time was different on a lot of levels, as I was coming to understand.

Conversation at the white linen table quickly arrived at the previous night's bump and grind across the lake in West Agave.

"A bunch of children, that's what they all are," Reed remarked between sips of his bottomless vodka tonic, which at this point I came to realize was more of an appendage than an accessory. "Some of us work for a living."

"And who would that be, dear?" Maisey chimed in.

Reed answered with a prolonged sip. "I heard rumors about the guy who bought the Linus Apple estate. Apparently he invented some videogame—Redo or Rehash..."

"Remake™?" I asked, a little too eagerly by the look Reed gave me.

"Something of the sort," he rolled his eyes. "They'll let almost anyone have a billion dollars these days."

Two of the houses' staff cleared the table and a couple more brought yet another course. They all looked vaguely Swedish and didn't speak.

"Apparently he's one of those whiz kids, dropped out of high school. He was in the news a while back." Reed seemed to glare at nothing in particular. "He has a funny name—Hoss or something."

"Joss," I said, putting it all together. He was the guy I saw reaching out his arms. That was Joss *fucking* Stember.

"What Joss?" Maisey suddenly perked up, more curious than I'd ever seen her.

Reed butts in before I could answer her. "It doesn't matter— new-new money comes and goes, it's anonymous, just like everything else in this disposable age." He took a drink and I looked over at Maisey who seemed as if she was trying to remember and forget something all at the same time. "There used to be a time when you knew your neighbors and your neighbors knew you. You may not have talked to each other, but you knew."

"He has an interesting story," I said absently.

"Old Sport," Reed addressed me, changing the subject. "I'm gonna take you riding today." He stood up like a man that had decided what he wanted to do for the rest of his life. "Have you ever ridden?"

"A motorcycle?" I asked hopefully.

He sneered. "No, my boy, a steed. A horse."

"I've, uh, never been too good with animals."

"Nonsense," Reed got out between sips. "Every man should know how to mount a beast."

"Every man should spend more time figuring out what to do once they mount it, if you ask me," Maisey mumbled.

$$$

I was sore as hell the next day. Apparently Reed came from the tough love school of riding. Despite my discomfort, I couldn't bear it any longer. Joss Stember was my neighbor. I had to go explore.

Skirting the edges of the lake, I peeked stealthily over the hedges that lined his property. I wanted in. This was too exciting—Joss Stember—the kid-billionaire recluse. In Linus Apple's old place! I read about him surfacing again. He was a trending topic for a couple days; and plastered across the supermarket aisles. Holy shit, this was too cool.

"Good afternoon," a voice came out of nowhere.

I turned around and standing ahead of me on the path not more than five feet away was the man himself. Joss Stember.

He looked every bit the mysterious figure he was. In a cream-colored suit that looked as if it had just been made that morning.

"Uh, sorry," I stammered. "I didn't see you."

"Quite alright," he said with a smile, extending his hand. "Joss Stember."

"Yes, I know," I said awkwardly.

He grinned uncomfortably.

"I'm Charlie Middle," I stammered.

"Yes," he said with a wink. "I know."

I looked at him, slightly confused.

"It's a small town, Charlie," he said gesturing towards Lake Agave. "You'll have to forgive me. I've been meaning to invite you over."

"Me?" I asked, even more confused now.

"I've seen you on your strolls, around the lake. I asked around. If you don't mind me saying, it seems you're a man who appreciates... being alone."

"Well, uh..."

I'm caught off guard by this whole exchange. *He'd seen me?* I had equal doses of adrenaline and pride.

"I'm someone who appreciates being alone as well," he added. "I've been meaning to invite you for a drink, so that we could maybe be alone... together."

"What about your party?" I asked. "How does someone who likes being alone throw a party like that?"

"You'd be surprised what one can do if he sets his mind to it." He gestured toward the house, skillfully changing the subject. "I noticed you taking a peek. Would you like a tour?"

I couldn't help but feel like he was an adult even though I knew he was only a few years older than me. Maisey's age actually. Although Joss seemed altogether different from Maisey. He knew exactly where he was supposed to be at all times. I always admired people who could be like that. I never knew exactly where I was supposed to be.

"I don't want to bother you," I started to say.

"I don't make a habit of doing things I don't want to do, Charlie." He opened a hidden gate in one of the hedges, revealing a set of railroad-tie steps. "These are from the tracks of the Orient Express," he said as we climbed up.

"Don't they need them?"

He laughed and led me up to the edge of the dock. I looked back across the lake and saw the lights of Maisey and Reed's house start to flicker on. The sun was almost over the mountain and the purple air carried with it a haze of magnolia and summer lawns. There was an orchestra of insects and amphibians that began to hum and I thought of the Tibetan monks that visited our school last April. They chanted for us, each of their different voices weaving in and out of each other in a wordless opera. I remember it sounding as if it were coming from a distant galaxy.

I turned and caught Joss gazing over at the house, too. And it occurred to me—that's exactly the direction he was facing when I first saw him, arms outstretched, reaching for something he could almost touch. He caught me staring at him, but his expression didn't change.

"Beautiful isn't it," he said rhetorically. There was a subtle nod of his head and an inside smile. "There's more here than one could ever know, Charlie."

"So I've heard," I answered.

Joss and I slowly serpentined our way through the old Apple Linus estate—Zen gardens with stones and sand imported from forbidden Japanese temples in the mountains of

Hokkaido, hedge mazes in the shape of supernatural fractals, swimming pools so pure you could drink from them, and a fortress of a house made of deep grey slate that looked as if it could double as an alien mothership from some distant galaxy.

We entered the residence through a stone staircase that led through a wine cellar the size of a Walmart.

"There are just as many vintages of Sake as there are Bordeaux," Joss let me know. "Linus was obsessed with Asian culture, particularly the Japanese."

We headed up a spiral staircase, made of tensile graphite as Joss pointed out. It seemed there was no detail left unremarked. Yet I had the feeling you could comb the house for decades and still not pick up on everything. Ornate is not the right word: there was a simplicity to the decadence. But it was decadence all the same. The rooms were sparse. But the detail and rich accentuation made it seem like adding a drop of furniture or anything more than was already there would be a crime against aesthetics. Tapestries that must be hundreds of years old and Samurai outfits standing sentry where, in some Anglo version of this house, you might see suits of armor.

"The whole Japanese thing never interested me before," Joss remarked. "But after spending the last several weeks here, it is undeniable. The silence. They knew what they were doing."

It took almost an hour to make it to the second floor. I didn't see any "staff" in the house, but somehow I knew they were there—blending into the slate walls and Japanese pastorals. The stone floors looked like they were constantly swept and the grounds were a symbol of inhuman perfection.

Joss looked back at me and gave an odd, almost guarded, gesture as he opened a set of carved double doors at the end of one of the many halls. There was a look of anticipation in his eyes, but a wariness in his manner. The room they led into was an Asian version of an old English study, less cavernous than most of the other rooms but more distinctive and grand somehow because of it. It didn't take me long to see that it was some kind of shrine. Pictures and newspaper clippings and random artifacts lining the walls. A memorial, I thought. I could make out a woman or a girl in a few of the photographs.

"Is that your mother?" I asked, approaching the sea of photos mounted on the wall. He didn't answer but as I worked out why the face looked so familiar, I froze. After a dissociative moment I whipped my head around and looked at Joss, a question mark plastered to my face. He had the glare of a seasoned poker player, guarded yet searching. I held his gaze for a few seconds and turned back to study the other photographs, trying to reconcile what was going on here.

Every photo, every newspaper clipping, were all of the same girl: Maisey.

"Joss," I said breathlessly. "I don't understand. You know Maisey?" He maintained his steady silence as I scrambled trying to take in everything. "I don't understand," I muttered absently, staring at a bleached-out shot of Maisey in front of an old Mustang convertible. After my confusion reached a certain pitch he dropped his guard, and laid down his hand.

"There's more here than one could ever know," he repeated the phrase he used earlier. But now it's almost as if he were asking a question. I guess there were red flags that popped up in my head, questions that I might have asked him. But I didn't pay any attention to those. I could have been much more suspicious, and perhaps I would have been if Joss were a mere mortal man—if these photos and news clippings had been in the basement of some modest home, taped crookedly to a water-stained wall. If that were the case I might have even thought about rushing home to call the police.

But it wasn't the den of a serial killer. And this wasn't a mortal man. This was Joss Stember: kid-billionaire, mysterious recluse, poster-boy for the iGeneration. And the care and attention that went into his tribute had the air of a temple or a museum, not a den of iniquity. Even so, I might have at least demanded an explanation. But instead, the first thing that came to my lips was a sly smile as my head shook in faux-disbelief.

"You're in love with Maisey," I said with a conspiratorial grin.

Joss gave the surprised smile of one who had expected a blow.

I spent time that night strolling along the wallpapered memories with Joss. Most were no more than a couple years old, with the exception of a few older photos and clippings: a preteen Maisey winning a middle school talent contest, tabloid articles about the bitter divorce of Maisey's parents, wedding photos. You couldn't say Joss wasn't thorough in his attempt to document her existence. And for my part, I took it all in like a tourist—ignoring any awkward feelings or sketchiness that I might have picked up. The way he was fully invested, the passionate story that he began to tell—how could I possibly do the disservice of questioning what this man had done? This was love, after all. And even if my only real experience on the subject was a few dark and desperate grope sessions and a penchant for tales of unrequited romance, I knew enough to know that I couldn't know enough. So all I said was, "wow."

I basked in the attention I was getting, the inside story that it was obvious had clearly stayed inside until now. I was special in the eyes of Joss, perhaps his only friend—his only *real* friend that is. He told me everything. The conspiratorial smile I had given him, in that moment when I had first realized Joss' secret, was all he needed. I was in. Inducted into a private army charged with taking the fortress on the other side of that imposing manmade lake, a bunker separating the false borders of class and civility. My mission, should I choose to accept it, was to rescue its most prized prisoner from the clutches of a life of rich mediocrity and drowned hope. Love was the battle call and sheer force of will was our armament. It was the most important I had ever felt and probably ever will.

I stood next to Joss on his dock, the same way my great-grandfather must have stood looking out at Normandy Beach in 1944. I said to myself: "this is my war." I could taste something bitter as I said the words, what I know now is the taste that every veteran of every war is never quite able to shed: the taste of death.

```
// ------------------------------------------------
----------------------------
     < p{margin: 4 error; "minimal}
   <a part="<of us got lost>"p{color: blue}
     </br>"<a#longform </br>
   <if"a" then>" match=.waypoint>
                             {black}=out
// ------------------------------------------------
----------------------------
```

"**D**ude, I could have predicted this," Anthony said, as Joss stared into his uneaten chili fries. "You've kept yourself wound so tight, you were bound to end up here."

"What are you talking about," Joss asked, eyes still cast downward as he sketched a question mark into the yellowish brown mush with one of his fries.

"Unless you've been holding out on me, you haven't so much as kissed a girl since Johnny-O's 8th grade graduation party." Anthony looked at Joss, nodding his head like a doctor reaffirming his diagnosis. "It's textbook stuff, man. After all that time with your dick bottled up, the first girl who's willing to bring it is gonna have you by the balls," he said as if it were a clinical diagnosis. "Literally and figuratively."

Joss' head sunk lower, and he let out a desperate sigh. "Dude, you don't understand. It isn't like that," he moaned. "It's..."

"It's different?" Anthony cut Joss off. "It always is, homey."

Joss looked up from his fries, but the intensity of Anthony's stare made him feel uneasy. "Whatever," Joss said bitterly, glancing away toward a couple sitting at another one of Tommy's cherry red tables.

Anthony raised his hands in a defensive posture. "Hey, don't shoot the messenger, man."

"It just doesn't make sense," Joss said over the traffic noise of Victory Boulevard. "I mean after all we've been through, you'd think she might have at least called."

"I don't want to be that guy, man," Anthony said apprehensively. "But you've only known each other for a few weeks."

"Six weeks," Joss corrected. "And we talked to each other every day. Every day, man. For hours. There was nothing we didn't know about each other."

"Dude," Anthony said, "first of all no matter how well you know a person, there's always secrets. Second of all, they think differently—the Richies. They have a whole different set of rules."

"Man, I told you she's not like the rest of them," Joss said, irritated. "Besides, that whole way of thinking is kinda bullshit. This isn't the dark ages. I mean her father came from nothing; she's second generation money. There's no reason that should make a difference."

"So why didn't she just come out and tell him?" Anthony snapped back. "If he's so understanding, if she's got nothing to hide? You said she was waiting to let him know until she got back to Cali. Why?"

Joss took a deep, exasperated breath and stared back down at his plate of uneaten food.

"Listen," Anthony continued. "Maybe she *is* different, maybe she *doesn't* subscribe to all the bullshit. But she's in it, whether she likes it or not. She's in a different world and so are you.

54

There's more distance between Reseda and Malibu than there is between here and London."

Anthony's words spun around Joss' head until they made him dizzy. Joss raised his hands as if to wave the words away, then froze in mid-gesture.

All of a sudden he looked up at Anthony. "That's it!"

"Uh oh," Anthony said looking worried.

"London *is* closer than Malibu. I can't believe it's taken three days to realize it." Joss began to stand up. "Anthony, thank you."

"Don't thank me for something I probably didn't even say. I don't like the look in your eyes, man," Anthony said warily.

"I have to go see her," Joss was standing now. "That's what she wants. It's what you're supposed to do," he declared. "That's the next scene of the movie. She wants me to rescue her."

"No, dude." Anthony held up his hand. "Bad idea."

"Oh, no," Joss corrected. "Good idea. Very, very good idea."

Anthony let his head fall into his hands in frustration and defeat. Joss hurried down the sidewalk calling back to him. "I'll see you in a few days, man. Thanks!"

All the way home Joss thought about how to tell his parents that he was just gonna pop over to jolly old England for a few days. He hadn't exactly mentioned the Joss Stember Fund to his parents. They might get weird. They would get weird. He had to just bite the bullet and call them when he landed in London.

He questioned whether it might not make more sense to get some perspective first. Then, after about five seconds, he stopped questioning. "This is what you do," he said to himself. "This is what you do." There was an electrical charge running through him and it felt like it could light the whole city. After visiting the bank and procuring a debit card linked to the $100,000 account, he used his mobile to purchase a last minute fare from eBay that set him back $975. He had stopped home for essentials: a change of clothes, his passport from an aborted trip to Vancouver last summer, the book of Maisey's letters he had been collecting, and the lucky rock he had pocketed from the beach their first night together.

The cab rolled through the Sepulveda corridor as if it were 3am instead of 3pm; even the traffic was on his side, he thought. He looked out the back window as the Valley disappeared behind him. The muddy gauze of smog, packed in like it's staunching a wound. To LA, The Valley is the low-rent, functioning alcoholic uncle who never gets invited to holiday dinners, but still comes. They were different worlds, Reseda and Malibu, Joss considered. But he and Maisey weren't bound by that kind of social geography.

The cab pulled up to the International Terminal and Joss leapt out. He was nearly through the sliding glass doors when the driver shouted in broken English, "Hey, you... You have to be paying me or I call the cops!"

It would be useful to bring his bag with all of his stuff, as well. He took a deep breath and said out loud, "Pull it together, man. Don't fuck this up."

Back at his house he had debated on whether he should bring his computer and decided against it, even though that was a form of heresy to a hacker. But as he stood in the security line, watching the TSA agents inspecting laptops like they were IEDs, he was glad he didn't. Not that they would have known necessarily, but there was some not-strictly-legal stuff on his hard drive. And with his luck he'd probably wind up in some back room of LAX, explaining to the FBI what Geezer's harmless file-bombing app, *I, Terrorist,* was all about. He breezed through security, and made his way to the gate. There was a delay, of course, and his plane wouldn't arrive for another two hours at least. Joss suddenly lamented not bringing his laptop. He hopped onto a rent-a-wreck computer terminal at one of the public kiosks and logged into his mail.

```
From: Landing, Brogan
To: Stember, Joss
Subject: Your Actions

Joss,

I thought we were clear, but apparently you
are too persistent for your own good. It is a
trait I usually admire, but unfortunately not
with my daughter's well being at stake. I
still don't hold this against you, Joss, but
you would be well served to look at how your
actions might affect those around you. Time
heals all wounds, while haste only makes them
deeper.

Yours,

Brogan Landing
```

The air escaped from his chest, and Joss stared down at his keyboard in utter confusion. His head popped up, surveying the neighboring gates like a deer that just heard the snap of a twig. The email—it was sent less than five minutes ago. How could he know? Was Landing having him followed? Or was it just coincidence? Joss reread the email, trying to reconcile what Landing meant by "Apparently you are too persistent for your own good." There was no way Landing could know he was at the airport. It was just really good timing. A coincidence, Joss tried to convince himself. You don't get to where Brogan Landing is without having one hell of an intuitive streak. Eyes on the prize, Joss reminded himself. He logged off the terminal, still a bit rattled, and decided to catch up on the sleep he'd missed over the last six years. To his surprise, he was able to nod off on a grouping of chairs next to his gate.

"Joss Stember?" An inhumanly deep voice startled him.

Joss sat up quickly. Two men in suits and sunglasses stood over him. "We don't want any trouble, son," one of them said in a voice calmer than he looked.

"No," Joss stuttered, holding a hand up in reassurance. He glanced curiously at the two men, who were holding out badges that said TSA. The one closest was Agent John Roberts.

"Am I not supposed to sleep on the chairs or something?" Joss asked, puzzled.

"Son, we need you to come with us for a few minutes so we can talk," the taller man, Roberts, said. They both wore dark suits with close-cropped hair. "Please," the second agent added.

"Is it Maisey?" Joss plead, not quite free of delirium yet.

They gave each other a confused look. "No, sir," Roberts assured him. "Please just come with us so we can talk in private."

Not sensing that he had a choice Joss picked up his bag and followed the men. As they passed through the terminal Joss noticed the darting eyes of all the other travelers walking by, glancing curiously at him and the two dark-suited agents. They rounded a bend past the restrooms. The unnamed agent punched in a key code on a door marked *no entry*. Joss was led down a slightly yellowed hallway through another door and into a white room with a mirror taking up the whole of one of the walls. Roberts pulled a chair out for Joss and the agents took seats on the other side of a large, rectangular table with a white Formica top. At first the agents didn't say anything. They just sat there with their palms pressed flat on the table looking at Joss with a cold, steady glare.

"I don't understand…" Joss asked tentatively after several seconds of silence. "Is there a problem?"

"Mr. Stember," Roberts said. "I have the duty to inform you that your name has been placed on the Transportation Security Administration's designated no-fly list. Your status will be placed on review following the protocol set forth in section 4, code 66X.129 of the US Flight Safety Security Manual. You have the right to appeal, in writing, should you choose."

"I don't understand," Joss said, wondering for a second if he might still be in a dream. "What did I do?"

"You are not currently under any criminal or jurisdictional investigation, however I do not have the clearance nor the obligation to say any more about that at this time. Your status as a no-fly passenger, Class B, precludes you from boarding any aircraft in the United States, or any aircraft bound for the United States. We regret the inconvenience this may cause you, and trust that you will work with TSA and its agents to resolve this matter in a timely fashion."

"Timely matter? What do you mean? I have a ticket for a flight to London that boards in an hour."

"I apologize for any inconvenience, Mr. Stember. Your ticket will be refunded minus a $100 handling fee within the next 6-8 weeks," Roberts said in a monotonous rasp.

"But I need to get to London," Joss pleaded. "How long will this take?"

"May we suggest you file an appeal for a speedy resolution?" Roberts said obligingly.

"Yes, definitely, where do I do that?"

"You can file a rush appeal in writing, postmarked on the first Monday of each fiscal quarter, except when preceded by a holiday, in which case the appeal must be filed on the preceding Monday. Except in the case of a Leap Year in which case the appeal must be filed on the Thursday prior."

"What?" Joss exclaimed. "How long does this usually take to get resolved?"

"A Rush Case is usually heard within the first 9 months of sanction," Roberts responded courteously.

Joss' whole body dropped.

"And then there is a review period of 6-8 months, followed by a processing period of 12-16 weeks."

"Just remember," the second agent assured Joss, who now had his head buried in his hands. "We're on your team."

"Can I pick a new team?" Joss mumbled.

They looked at him crookedly.

"Just kidding."

A few minutes later, Joss oozed out of the airport and took the first cab he could find. It took half the evening to inch through the rush hour gridlock. And when he finally arrived home, battered and broken, he slunk into his room, shut the shades and fell into a deep troubled sleep.

Ding. His email alert woke him and he looked around disoriented. 12:55am, according to his bedside clock. He stared up for a few blurry minutes, trying to discern whether it was all a dream. It wasn't. He banged his right leg on the side of his desk as he got up and clinched in pain. He reached for his laptop and pulled it onto the bed, not even bothering to assume his normal position on the floor. Clicking the alert brought him into his Gmail account, where there was a message waiting. Joss had to stare at the subject line and sender before he believed what he was looking at, and even then it took him at least a minute of breathless, stomach-retching anticipation before he summoned the nerve to click it open.

```
From: Landing, Maisey
Subject: Please Stop

Joss,
I thought my father made it clear, but I
realize now that you probably have to hear it
from me to believe it. First of all, what we
had was magical. Clearly there was something
there between us that neither of us could
deny. But I am torn apart right now and need
to be alone. It was a mistake that we made,
one that I now have to pay for. We tried,
Joss. But we are from different worlds and as
much as we might not want to admit it, there
will always be a divide. Please understand
that as short as it was, this is the closest I
have felt to love. But after all is said and
done, that isn't enough.

-Maisey
```

"You're fucking kidding me," Joss said through an oncoming sob that he tried his best to keep at bay. "Different worlds?" He attempted to reason his way out of this: this isn't Maisey, he said. It's her father. He did this. But Joss knows Maisey's writing too well. Even if he didn't believe what she was saying, he recognized the way she was saying it. "Could I actually have been that blind?" he said out loud.

He stared blankly into space and, after a few minutes, picked up his cell. "You were right," he texted Anthony. "I didn't go."

"I didn't want to be," Anthony's reply came back almost right away. "Let's hang tomorrow, brother. Blow off some steam. It's summer time, baby!"

$$$

Joss did spend the balance of the summer blowing off steam, enough of it to power the entire industrial age. Never a drinker or partier or player before, Joss made up for it over the next set of weeks, and then some. "Dude, you see that girl," Joss said to Anthony at a random Fourth of July party somewhere in Encino.

"Yeah. Man," Anthony said half-heartedly. He felt culpable for Joss' descent, but hadn't been able to find a way to get him out of the nosedive he was taking.

"She's got a bulls-eye tattoo on her back, with a dollar sign right in the center." Joss was seven beers in and it was only 4pm. "I'm gonna go in for some target practice. I'll see you in the morning." Joss handed his empty cup to Anthony, who just shook his head.

By late July, Joss had blown off Anthony and the rest of the gang completely, choosing instead to travel with a wolf pack from Alemany High dedicated to targeting all the Richie girls they could. Search and destroy.

His parents were never home, therefore they couldn't really track the descent Joss was making. Mr. and Mrs. Stember were busy taking on extra-overtime to get a head start on Joss' college fund—one year away and counting. Joss had failed to mention to them the generous grant from Brogan Landing. He'd actually almost forgot about it himself. Short of the $100 handling fee assessed when his London ticket was returned, he hadn't spent any of it. Jake was already in Berkeley, training with the team, so he couldn't see what was happening. The only person that could have helped Joss was Joss, and he wasn't around that summer either.

An email alert dinged Joss awake on the Sunday morning before school started. It took him a groggy minute before he decided he couldn't get back to sleep. He studied himself in the mirror. His hair still slicked back from the night before but crooked in a few spots. The clothes that he had been wearing for the last three days clung to his body for dear life. Each of his limp eyes hung just above a pool of bruised darkness that had been there for most of the last month. He smelled of stale beer and whatever girl he had been with the night before. He tried to remember: was it Bianca or Taylor or... *Ashley*, that's it, it was Ashley—the name that Maisey almost got branded with. He was proud of that one. Although pride isn't the word. Joss didn't know what the exact word was. Maybe there wasn't one.

Joss took a breath and then picked up the Gatorade next to his laptop and checked for the email alert. But it wasn't an email alert. It was a Google news alert, which confused Joss until he opened it. He had set it up when he was still wondering where Maisey had vanished to, in those first few days before he woke up to reality. His hand shook as he tried to steady it enough to click on the link.

DAUGHTER OF MEDIA MOGUL BROGAN LANDING TO WED VENTURE CAPITALIST HEIR REED GRAFT

Century City, CA - In an announcement certain to roil the leagues of media pundits and Silicon Valley companies alike, Maisey Landing and Reed Graft will be wed in a small ceremony at the Graft family estate. "We are excited about the prospect of new media ventures, but we are even more excited to celebrate the happiness of our daughter and our new son," Brogan Landing commented as reporters immediately pounced on the prospect of

63

potential merger rumors. Mr. Landing was joined by his future son-in-law, Reed Graft outside the offices of his Beverly Hills complex. Reed Graft's father, Robert Graft, recently deceased, founded Legacy Partners, the world's largest and oldest Venture Capital firm. Maisey Landing was not present at the press conference, and was unavailable for comment by phone or email.

Sparks shot through Joss' fingertips as if the news itself was sending a current through his computer into his body. He raised his hands and stared at them, then back down at the screen. Emotions began to flood in his chest so quickly he couldn't keep track of them—anger, pain, shame, heartache—It was a cacophony of colors that when mixed together made a dull, brown gray. This was it, Joss thought: the final nail in the coffin. The whole summer, all that time he had invested in trying to bury the pain, was for shit. It all came bubbling up, now, right back to that moment in early June when he first read Maisey's email declaring her independence from him.

Sobs breached the hold of his chest. Then his throat clenched and he began a slow, wailing moan. He ripped the parachute shades off the window and the sunlight seared him as if he were a porcelain-skinned vampire boy. He didn't care—he just kept ripping things off the wall, off his bed, off his desk.

Ding. Another news alert, he assumed, and crouched over his computer to mainline some more pain. But it wasn't a news alert. It was an email.

"Holy shit," he whispered, as he clicked through.

From: Anonymous
To: Stember, Joss
Subject: The Canyon

It is a lie, all of it. But it is a lie we are
forced to tell.

Don't think of this as a cry for help, my sweet one. And do not reply or come after me. I'm not there, and I never will be. This is not a movie, and if it is there's no happy ending. You won't be able to save me at the altar. This is real life and real life is full of things that are fake.

Don't forget about me, though. Maybe just put some flowers on the side of the road, in the place I ended up going over.

Your lady of the canyon,
M

Joss closed the email. He let the steam that had been bottled inside his body escape from the cracks that were now, finally, broken open: the rank smell of summer, the bitter taste of heartbreak, the realization of a world that existed beyond his control. It all came hissing out and in one vaporous trail and made its way though a crack in the window.

Joss saw himself in the reflection of his monitor. He had been gone so long that he hadn't even noticed he was missing. He breathed in the perfumed scent of Maisey's email, it permeated his room. It made everything good again. In its total lack of hope, it offered a hope that he couldn't quite explain.

Joss knew what he had to do. It was a moment of clarity that opened up like the dawn of that first morning he spent with Maisey. He saw each color and could describe it in a glorious detail. He saw where the sun was rising and worked out where it would set. He placed the coordinates in his mind. He judged the speed at which he needed to travel. He could do it, he realized. He could get there. And if he was lucky, he just might be able to beat the sun before it had a chance to set.

CHAPTER SEVEN

"They're here," Joss said, glancing toward the house.

"Who's here?"

"Well," he had a childish grin. "I had a lot of complaints, after that last party. So, I talked to this executive at NASA who needed a favor." He looked at me and paused.

"What," I urged him on.

"I'm having sonic soundproofing installed."

"Excellent," I said, with the oversized enthusiasm expected of a right hand man. I paused. "Joss, what exactly is sonic soundproofing?"

"It's a sub-audio frequency capacitor that will contain almost any level of decibels within a specified region."

"Uh..."

"It puts the party on mute for the neighbors, but not the guests."

"Whoa... I... I didn't know that was possible... NASA?" I said in disbelief.

"We'll see if it actually works outside of a lab, it's still a prototype. But I thought it would be a useful pretext for inviting my neighbors to next Saturday's event."

At first I just looked at him confused, but then I followed his gaze over to the Graft estate. "Oh," I said, finally getting it.

"An olive branch," he smiled. "You think you could handle your end?" he asked, expecting me to know that he meant getting the Grafts to attend.

I knew exactly what he meant, though. And gave a tight nod as if accepting orders.

$$$

A few days later, the Tuesday before the party, I was lying on my much-too-comfortable bed, staring at the ceiling. It was made up of white tiles depicting scenes of pre-civil war Southern life.

"Maisey," I said into the receiver of the house phone.

"Charlie Middle," she answered back in her impossible, breathy voice. "It's simply been ages, where have you been!"

"Walking the waterfront," I played along.

"I think I saw you there," she said, as if she were an old-time actress. "Through a foggy window and a heart of glass."

"I wanted to ask you a question."

"Charlie Middle is this a quiz," she asked playfully.

"More of a conspiracy," I hazarded.

"Conspiracy!" she said with glee. "That's my absolute favorite thing. How did you know?"

"Lucky guess?"

"Charlie Middle, you are one of the best things to happen to me in my entire short life."

"I want you to make a fake date for this Saturday," I said in my most clandestine voice.

"What is a fake date," she begged with childish abandon. "Is this a Midwest thing like tipping sheep?"

"No, it's not a Midwest thing. And it's cows, not sheep."

"Well wouldn't have I been embarrassed?"

"Maisey, I need you to cancel any previously scheduled event. I have a party I want to take you guys to, but I want it to be a surprise."

"A surprise?" Maisey rasped. "Whose party is it, will there be revolutionaries and royalty?"

"That's too deep in the conspiracy for you right now, Maisey. It's on a need-to-know basis, at this point."

"Oh, that's so not fair," she protested. "I object!"

"That's how this kind of stuff works."
"You mean we all get screwed in the end," she asked.

I let the words sit there—afraid to touch them but unable to look away. "Yes," I finally answered. "And that's if we're lucky,"

$$$

Saturday night rolled around and the Graft's fake engagement fell through as planned. Maisey, Reed and I went to Palo Alto for dinner instead. On our way home James took the West Agave turnoff, instead of the East.

"James," Reed asked, raising his voice to be heard from the back seat. "Did you get high in the parking lot or are you taking the scenic route?"

68

"It's not him," I leaned forward and turned to Reed, readying my offense. "I asked him to... I have a surprise."

Reed squinted at me, as if he now wondered who the hell I was. "I don't think I understand, Charlie."

I smiled like a wide-eyed innocent. "I'm taking you to a party," I said in a playful chirp. "The same party from two weeks ago."

He had a curdled look on his face like he just smelled something horrible. "Someone's been having a party for two weeks straight?"

What a lunkhead, I said to myself. "No the same place where the party was two weeks ago. They invited all the neighbors, as a way to make up for all the complaints."

Reed continued staring at me with an unpleasant look.

"I ran into the guy who hosts the parties on one of my walks around the lake," I continued, hewing as close to the truth as I could. "He felt bad about the noise and has this NASA soundproofing device installed." I roll down the window. "Listen."

Reed stuck his head out the window and back in again. "I don't hear a thing," he said as if disproving my claim.

"That's the point," I said, trying to be patient. "Just wait."

We approached and you could see the neon pulses and rainbow lasers explode out of the approaching distance. It was as if the ravers of the world were firebombing the tree line with Day-Glo napalm.

"It's simply divine," Maisey said, sticking her head past Reed and out through the window."

"I don't see any harm in driving by but we're not going in," Reed said shaking his head like a disappointed parent. "This is just not how we Grafts do things, Charlie."

"Oh stop it, Reed," Maisey complained. "Charlie is just trying to take us out for some fun. He let you nearly break his neck with your silly ponies, the least you can do is indulge him."

Reed furrowed his brow and continued shaking his head. "I'll indulge him," he looked at me suspiciously. "I'll indulge you, Charlie. Even if I don't know what the hell you're up to."

"I just wanted to do something else than stay in the house," I said in my best *aww shucks*, Midwest affect. "I wanted us to have some fun, like Maisey said."

He looked me squarely in the eyes. "I can tell after seven seconds, if you've been lying," he said unblinking. "It's proven. Learned from a paramilitary expert that served in wars no one even knows about."

He stared at me for several seconds, wordlessly. Out of the corner of my eye I could see Maisey roll her eyes. "Well, am I lying?" I asked him, getting nervous.

"No," he took a deep breath and blinked, shaking himself off. "Sorry, it takes a lot out of me every time I use it." He looked like a TV preacher, post-sermon.

"Of course," I said placating.

He looked at me defensively. "Are you being droll?"

"No," I demanded, clenching my teeth. "That's amazing. I mean, you got it right, I *was* telling the truth."

After a long pause he shook his head and smiled, taking on a prideful glow. We pulled toward the mile long driveway and all of a sudden a blanket of sound enveloped us. Reed decided we should put the top down to be able to hear the change when we passed the sound barrier. And when it did hit, it was like an avalanche.

"Is this sonic insulation dangerous in any way," Maisey shouted over the sudden deluge.

I shrugged my shoulders and grinned, "probably less dangerous than the music itself."

There were lines of cars clogging the driveway, so James stopped and let us out to walk. We crossed the vast expanse of lawn, dotted with small rock gardens, as the sound of cheers and a thump-thump-thump-thump permeated the air around us. "Whoa," Reed exclaimed, before catching himself and returning to his perpetual state of indifference. Maisey and I looked at each other in wonder. It sounded like we were in a club or a studio; the sound was so tight and acoustically tuned. I hadn't considered that value of the sonic insulation. Despite my earlier concern, Reed was starting to go with it. He saw the cars of some of his friends and rattled off a few names like he was taking social inventory. "Why didn't we get invited to this?" He asked Maisey as we made our way across the lawn.

"We did," she reminded him. "We had that prior engagement."

"Oh well," he said blithely, as if trying to get us to lighten up. "We're here now; we might as well suck it up and make the best of it."

"You're such a trooper, dear." Maisey rolled her eyes and turned to me with her *help me* look. The three of us made our way up the front steps and entered through twenty-foot tall Japanese castle doors. They opened to an entryway offering a portal the size of a football field to the backyard. Fifty-foot slate walls that by day were the zenith of understated elegance now served as the broad canvas for a light and laser show that was deceptive in its subtlety. So captivating that even the most jaded partygoers were transfixed as they made their way through the grand hallway and out to the back yard.

"There's the Gundersons," Reed said, feigning a cool boredom. "I can't believe the Van Tufts actually came... Oh, God, she *has* gained weight. Pity."

Maisey on the other hand walked through the hall transfixed, like a child entering the gates of a theme park.

Reed put a hand over his eyes as if to block a non-existent glare, "Is that Tom Parker?" He looked to Maisey for recognition but she was lost in the lights. "Honey I have to go say hello."

"That's quite alright," she answered without looking at him. "Charlie and I want to escape you anyway."

He laughed as if that were the least likely thing ever. "I'll catch up. Have fun kids."

"Thanks daddy," she said tartly. Maisey nearly ripped my arm out of its socket, pulling me through the hall and out to the backyard. There were tiers of people to the left and right, forward and backward, thousands of them. And three separate "invisible tents" with people dancing to distinctly different BPMs. Each "tent" was contained by smaller sonic insulators, which confined the three different soundtracks playing in each of them to their respective dance floors.

"Sonic Tents," I marveled.

One was obviously a chill tent from the way the guests seemed to float along the dance floor as if they were in zero gravity. The other looked like it must have been a harder driving soundtrack, perhaps even punk or metal the way the people were jumping up and down and into each other. The third was harder to pin down from here.

Maisey pulled me onto the main dance floor, which was uncontained and pumped out the music we had been hearing since we arrived. It was set up like a spaceship on the terrace above the other three, which were all positioned as booster rockets. The DJ on the main dance floor was mixing at least three different songs I recognized, all at the same time, along with a few I didn't recognize. Before I could react, I was dancing. And I actually didn't mind. This wasn't the case most of the time—I usually didn't go to places where you were expected to dance. But I *was* dancing, and I couldn't give a shit how I looked cause I felt liberated. Flesh pressed up against flesh, it felt like an orgy. And it basically was. I made out with three different women who probably would never give me a second look if they saw me on the street.

It was Maisey who after about forty-five minutes signaled me to take a break. "Come with me Charlie Middle," she shouted over the music. "I need to get a drink. And so do you."

I followed her through the growing, twisting mass of people that pulsed from the epicenter of the DJ booth. Bodies sprawled out to the edges of the main floor as if they were one gigantic organism with several hundred moving parts. I felt connected and free at the same time. We snaked through the crowd as if we were being squeezed through, and when we shot out the back it made me think that I'd just been digested. And in a way, I had.

Maisey and I made our way to a grassy knoll by the edge of the property, where the population was thinned out significantly. "Holy smokes, Midwest, "Maisey laughed, lighting up a cigarette and taking a hit off a pink flask she pulled from her square metal purse. "You know how to move." I took a swig from the flask as well, and we repeated the cycle several times.

Before I knew it I was smoking a cigarette, which I couldn't remember doing since that one time in 7th grade behind the Mi-T-Mart.

We laid back on the grass taking drags from each other's hands. "Do you think the moon exists," I asked, absolutely sloshed. Mr. zero-tolerance.

"I believe in the moon more than I believe in my own reflection," she said dreamily.

I gazed at the starry blanket above and tried to make a wish, but couldn't think of anything to wish for. "I know you're not happy, Maisey," I whispered, almost to myself. There was no response. "I also know that you deserve to be," I pressed on, lightly. "You deserve to have someone who worships you."

Maisey gave a tearful chuckle, "Charlie Middle, you are so filled with Midwest optimism."

"I sort of did something," I said feeling a little stoned. "But I think it was the right thing to do."

"You're drunk as a skunk, Charlie Middle," she pulled a few blades of grass from the summer lawn and tossed them in my face. "What are you talking about?"

I got up to a sitting position and found myself spinning less than I had predicted. I got up all the way and extended my hand to Maisey.

"What for?" she said stubbornly.

"For the hell of it," I answered.

"Now *that's* a cause I can get behind." She took my hand and I gently lifted my second cousin to her feet. We locked arms and made our way down to the lake. After stumbling more than once we approached the jetty where I had first seen Joss looking out upon the water. A couple staggered off the dock and crookedly navigated their way back to the party. Maisey tightened her grip on my hand and began walking, breathlessly, on the wood planks of the pier. She was so quiet and uncharacteristically tense. She must have suspected something. Each step seemed to hover in the air before it landed. And her hand was warm and soft in mine, until at the last minute she let go.

There was a figure at the end of the dock, standing on the edge of a shadow cast by the dropping light of a dim lamppost. Maisey and I halted, several feet short of him as if we were in a movie, about to trade hostages or collect ransom. Seconds tiptoed past and the silence threatened to cave in on us.

"Is it really you?" she said in a steady, empty plea.

"I think so," Joss answered.

"Do you look different?" She took a measured step forward. "I can't see your face."

"I don't know."

"Do I look different?" she asked, as if it were a question she was posing to herself.

"Not one bit," he answered, stepping out of the shadow. A breath escaped her lips, somewhere between a moan and a sigh. Maisey took a step and he matched it—each of them moving inexorably closer to the other until they didn't so much embrace, as simply come together. And in a feat of magnetic grace their bodies fastened to one another. The hot breath of alcohol, like incense in a lover's den, spun around like a potion above their heads. Every part of them was touching at that point—sealed in a kiss that seemed so overpowering it was hard to believe it was human.

I looked around anxiously, half expecting Reed to pop out at any moment. And after a minute of feeling awkward, I began to sneak away down the jetty.

"You're not going anywhere, Charlie Middle," Maisey reprimanded me, tearing herself away from their embrace to cut off my escape route.

I froze. Maisey walked over to secure me and Joss was left standing like a cartoon character who'd just been hit over the head with a sledgehammer. Maisey refused to look back at him, and suddenly had a defensive air about her. "It's funny, you buying a property here in Agave," she said to him, her eyes still locked on to mine. "Location, location, location, I guess." She took a shallow breath and gestured around at the house, the party, everything. "Is this your way of preening your fancy peacock feathers, Joss Stember? Did you come to buy me," she choked up. There was a battle being waged inside her eyes. "Did you think you could?" She held my gaze as if using it to steady herself.

Joss was silent, tense and unsure what to say even though he'd thought this out an infinite amount of times—in his head and on paper—every possible way but the right way.

"I have been looking for you," his breath trembled.

Her gaze reluctantly peeled off of me and fell back onto Joss.

"I have been waiting... for so long, Maisey," he continued breathlessly. "For so long."

You could tell he wanted to say more but the words wouldn't come. It was painful to watch him try and lift them. There was a petrified moment that stretched out too long. I stepped forward to say something, anything—afraid that the world might suck us in and trap us here in this moment if I didn't do something to fill the void.

Before I could, though, Maisey walked over to Joss, gently brushed the hair from his eyes and pulled him into a soft, bottomless embrace.

"You found me," she said, peering over his shoulder at the distant lights of the Graft estate. "Now what?"

CHAPTER EIGHT

```
#import self

#import "extensions.h"

// ----------------------------------------------
----------------------------
// p{margin 16pt "What is the perfect way to
answer a question?"}
// ----------------------------------------------
----------------------------
-
// container isn't by default
    }
    return self;
}

// ----------------------------------------------
----------------------------
// if "line" textA=always "skipB"container

p{margin 16pt "Make sure the right one gets asked."
WAN/Y}
// ----------------------------------------------
----------------------------
```

"What are you doing, dude?" Anthony asked in disbelief. "I watched you go down once before and felt like I couldn't do anything. But I'm not gonna let that happen again, man."

Joss should have been out of his house fifteen minutes ago. He was going to be late picking up Geezer and Klondike, his hacker friends that had flown in from London thanks to a generous contribution from the Brogan Landing Fund. If he wasn't at LAX on time, who knows where they'd end up. Probably not somewhere very reputable, Joss thought.

"Remake™," Joss said, smiling like Anthony hadn't seen him smile in months.

"What?"

"That's what it's called, what I'm working on: Remake."

"Man, I'm glad you're back from Zombieland, but you can't just drop out of school for some weird idea," Anthony demanded.

"I'm not just dropping out of school," Joss answered, doing a final inventory of paperwork and folders wallets and cash. "I took the GED yesterday," he smiled theatrically, zipping up his bag. "They said they had rarely, if ever, seen such a score," Joss said with mock pride.

"Yeah, that's because only dropouts take the GED!" Anthony retorted. "Listen, your mom and dad are freaking out, and they're right."

"I know," Joss sighed as if he didn't need to be reminded of that unfortunate side effect. "They'll get over it, though. Trust me."

"Joss, man… They've worked their whole life for you. Every fucking overtime eighty-hour week was for you. And now you're just gonna shit that away, right on their doorstep?"

"Anthony," Joss said calmly but matter-of-factly. "I love and respect them more than you can know. And the same goes for you. But you guys are gonna have to trust me, even if my lost summer might have left some doubts about my sanity." He zipped his laptop into his bag and gestured Anthony out the door. "The only deadly thing I'm still into is Tommy's chili fries."

Anthony shook his head.

Joss patted himself down and took one final inventory then headed out his bedroom door, ducking under the chin up bar. "Come on, I'm late."

Anthony gave a defeated sigh and trailed Joss out the door.

$$$

Joss had logged so many vid chat hours with Geezer and Klondike over the last year that he had probably spent more face time with them than his own family. But when he saw them walk out of the International terminal at LAX, he almost didn't recognize them. Even though they were impossible to miss.

Klondike was much shorter than Joss would have ever guessed, five four at the most. Some things just don't translate online, even over video. He had pasty white skin and a shock of red hair, not reddish like Joss's, but bright red. He dressed in a purple suit that, along with the hair, made him look like The Joker. He walked like he talked, bouncy and jittery, jacked up on caffeine and inflated with an IQ that was off the charts.

Geezer was his polar opposite--except for the intelligence quotient—skinny as a rail and dressed completely in black, with spiky-dyed hair to match. He had drawn a single white line across the bottom of his left eye that contrasted perfectly with his dark skin. His face was hollowed out but he looked alive rather than undead. It was hard to tell age on these guys, but he was a few years older than Klondike, around twenty-four. He had so many piercings it looked as if he couldn't take a drink without springing a leak.

Geezer had a spark, though, which was one of the things that *did* come through over vid chat and even texts. He was unquestionably Joss' biggest cheerleader, spending countless hours and data bits walking Joss through computer language and binary systems that it seemed Joss would never get. But Geezer never waivered, and because of that Joss had not given up. Joss owed him big-time for that, for giving him the skills that just might allow Joss a way forward, through the milky haze of heartbreak to the place where his prize was being kept.

"Bloody Hell, Joss," Klondike belted in a voice that seemed way too big for his body. "You look like a fucking wanker in person." He took off his oversized heart-shaped sunglasses to get a better look at Joss. Every one in the loading area was staring at them. They probably thought Geezer and Klondike were rock stars. And the thing is they sorta were.

"Piss off then," Geezer shoved Klondike. "You look brilliant, mate," Geezer said walking toward Joss with arms outstretched. They both descended on Joss for a hug.

"Man, I can't believe you're here, " Joss gleamed. "Thank you guys, so much."

"No worries, mate," Geezer shook his head as if to say thank *you*.

"Yeah, I bloody well can't stand London, anymore," Klondike added. "Especially with that fascist regime and all the CCTV bullocks."

"Well, I'm glad the student visa idea worked," Joss said. "Still, we have a lot to do in a short amount of time."

"So let's get on with it then," Geezer said, leading the charge.

"We *are* going to get hookers first, though, right?" Klondike added.

"Bloody hell," Geezer slapped Klondike's arm, as Joss tried to decipher whether he was serious or not. "You couldn't get laid in a mattress shop."

"Didn't you see that fit bird staring at me the whole flight?"

"Yeah I saw her," Geezer turned to address Joss. "She was wondering whether K-Dike was my little boy or not."

"Toss off," Klondike said as they loaded up the car.

"Move along." An airport cop shouted at us from down the curb. "No loitering."

"What's it look like we're doing, then," Klondike barked back.

"Dude," Joss elbowed Klondike, still smarting from his last experience at LAX. "Don't fuck with the airport police. They have more pull than the CIA."

"Yeah, they'll be the first up against the wall when the whole mess blows," Klondike muttered.

"Forgive him, Joss," Geezer said. "He's been reading too much anarchist literature of late."

"Yeah, you'll see," Klondike shook his head and gave Joss a knowing wink. "Remember, remember, the fifth of November."

Joss muscled through the mid-day traffic, headed north on the 405 to a live/work loft Joss had leased for them on the cheap. Things were in motion. Decisions were made. And Joss knew that he hadn't gotten all of them right. But he hoped he'd guessed right on the things that really mattered. Even if he didn't know what those things were.

$$$

"We both understand what it does," Geezer said, sipping on a Gin and Juice. Snoop Dogg's classic track blasted from the speakers inside the crumbling loft. "We just don't understand why. I mean it's a brilliant trick you've got there, Joss. It's just..." he trailed off.

"What's the fucking point?" Klondike said without the inhibitions Geezer seemed to have.

"Money," Joss said without a hint of irony.

They both looked at him, trying to figure out whether he was messing with them.

"This may be just a clever bit of code to you guys," Joss said pacing back and forth. "But if we can get the functionality in place and work up the right kind of UI, and fix some of the bandwidth issues, we can turn it into more than just a simple app that goes viral on Facebook. We can turn it into a way that people communicate with each other."

Klondike stared around the room uncomfortably and Geezer nudged him.

"If we take this to the media companies and show them how it works…" Joss caught his breath. "Show them they can use it as a built-in viral advertising tool that doesn't even seem like advertising to the people who use it. It'll be like a Trojan Horse of marketing for them. All the users will just be having fun, putting each other into the vid feed into whatever the meme of the moment is. Any line they want them to say."

"So it's all about money then," Geezer asked, clearly disappointed.

"Yes," Joss declared, looking them square in the eyes.

Klondike turned up his face in disgust.

"And no," Joss added with emphasis.

"What then," Geezer asked skeptically.

Joss looked at the floor for a moment, then stared Geezer dead in the eye.

"Love."

CHAPTER NINE

"You have to understand, Charlie Middle." Maisey was staring into her glass, as if she were trying to read her own fortune. "The easy life can sometimes be the hardest life of all."

We sat out on a sprawling balcony off the second floor of the Graft estate, drinking and eating, looking out onto Lake Agave and over to the old Linus Apple estate. I didn't think Maisey wanted me to say anything, so I just nodded uncertainly.

"Joss and I were so in love when we met." She lit a cigarette. "I'm sure he's told you. And whatever fanciful, impossible notions he spoke of having, however hard it is to believe--given our young, unpracticed hearts--it was all true."

She took my hand in hers, the way she always did. My feelings for her were so complicated: this playful, illicit lust always running through my bloodstream, which she does her best to feed. But more than that there was a pain that I felt—a contact pain—a pain that's epicenter was her heart.

"I won't bore you with the details of our courtship or the hours we spent back and forth through the ethers, falling in love every day, over and over again."

I gestured toward her pack of cigarettes, and she pushed it toward me.

"I hope I'm not corrupting you too horribly, Charlie Middle. I hope you'll always stay pure. Pure as the Midwest snow."

I half-smiled. "I'll live."

"You will, indeed, Charlie Middle. A long happy life," she gave me the saddest smile I'd ever seen as she lit my smoke.

"Perhaps Joss spoke of how we lost touch. It was quick and violent, to say the least. But he doesn't know the whole story. Maybe no one does." She looked at me, trying to steel herself.

"My father came to visit and I'd been feeling ill, a bug or something. We went to a family doctor in London who let us know, unceremoniously, that I was pregnant. First time's a charm, I guess," she said with a broken smile. Maisey took a drag and let out a long, slow exhale. "His rage was muted only by the fact that the doctor was there. 'I want to keep it,' I said foolishly, 'I'm in love.' This of course only freaked him out more. He forced the doctor to sedate me and by the time I awoke, I was no longer *with child*."

I couldn't keep the horror from creeping into my features. Maisey gave me a tight nod.

"That business done," she continued after a brief, shuddering silence, "my father proceeded to tell me exactly what was to happen from there: I would not be going home for the summer, I was not to have contact with Joss ever again, and I would continue the summer in Paris—where he would see to it that I had an internship at *Paris Vogue*. He spoke of it all as if he were giving me the opportunity of a lifetime. 'Second chances don't come cheap' I remember him saying. I resisted, of course. I ran away. More than once. But he is an octopus, his tentacles far-reaching. He had me apprehended at Gatwick airport, twenty minutes before my plane to LAX."

"Maisey," I said, stunned into silence, but eager to console. "I'm so sorry... I just... I just can't imagine."

She waved it off. "There are some imaginations one is better off not acquiring, Charlie Middle."

She let me take her hand.

"Anyway, I continued to resist and sensing that I wouldn't easily be contained, my father had me checked into rehab. Glengarry Roses, such a quaint name for such a horrific place. He even had that shitbag doctor make a recommendation, which made my stay there mandatory."

She finished her drink, poured another and grinded out the rest of the story, like a haggard veteran of a forgotten war.

"It was the final straw, as they say. It broke me in half, and everything that was pure and good and full of hope leaked out of me as if I were a cracked vase. The rest of my stay was a blur, and when I finally got out, I was in such a stupor that I didn't even resist the marriage my father had constructed.

She looked at me, arching her eyebrows. Both of our cigarettes were down to butts, and I watched her flick a tiny spark onto the perfect grass.

"I sleepwalked in to the life you now see. Half a life, as it were." She reached for another cigarette. "Poor little fool," Maisey half-sung to herself. "Poor little, rich fool."

"You have to tell someone," I said, indignant. "We can bring your father up on charges. You were a *minor*." I struggled to keep in my seat.

She laughed, a harsh crackle.

"Oh, pure Charlie Middle. There is nothing to be done. There is no charge that can be brought. You don't get to where my father is without knowing your way around everything. I couldn't escape." Her gaze fell across the lake to the old Linus Apple estate. "Even if I wanted to."

"Maisey, I just... I need to do *something*," I pleaded.

"You can't undo the past. And you can't put it back together either." She fixed me with a critical gaze. "If you tell Joss, if you tell anyone, I would be heartbroken all over again. Whatever good you think you might be doing for me would only come back to strike us, and tenfold the worse."

I nodded in silent, reluctant agreement. I couldn't find anything to do with my hands and I felt like I was about to burst into tears. I thought about how Joss was even now probably looking through some high-powered NASA binoculars that could listen in to our conversation. I felt ill.

"So." Maisey shifted in her chair. "What exciting things do we have on the calendar for today. Let's banish this darkness and go shopping in the city! Spending money is the best form of therapy one can find," she assured me with a hollow smile. I took her outstretched hand.

$$$

Over the next couple weeks, Maisey and Joss worked out their rendezvous to a science, using me to great effect. I was the ultimate middleman—in name and form. Always finding a way to disappear into the background or hide in plain sight. At first Maisey treated me as one would a set of training wheels, but soon she was riding all on her own. They dove into each other, body and soul, seeming to pick up right where they left off.

"How did you do it?" Maisey's eyes were closed and her head rested carefree in Joss' lap. The three of us sat on a windy beach, staring at the Golden Gate Bridge. I felt as if I was an invisible spectator. "How did you climb up so high, so quickly, my love," she continued, as if she were auditioning for a role.

Joss ran his fingers lightly through her gently curled sunshine, the afternoon sun making everything seem like an old washed out photo. "I didn't climb, I just lowered the ladder," he said with a confident smile.

Maisey blinked, as if an unhappy thought had just crossed her mind. "Despite what we share, we always tend to keep the most important things for ourselves," she said, challenging him.

"The most important things don't belong to us," Joss whispered as he leaned down and placed his lips on each of Maisey's eyelids. "They are not ours to give or keep. They are only ours to share."

"Fancy talk coming from a billionaire," Maisey jested playfully.

Joss didn't waiver. "There were a billion steps on the stairway," Joss whispered, rolling her over on her back, pinning her arms in the sand, gently placing his lips to her chest then neck. His fingers walked up Maisey's golden thighs and her head tilted back involuntarily. "I took each of them one by one, knowing that eventually they would lead to you."

"My brave soldier," she cooed, eyes closed in a carnal trance.

It was as if I wasn't there. You could see something in her change, another person take over. All the talk stopped and I sat there ten feet away not knowing what to do with myself. The thought that they may have wanted me to see this for some reason scared me more than anything else. Part of me wanted to see them falling deeper and deeper into each other, if only for proof that we were winning the battle. But most of me felt the uncomfortable shame of a voyeur. So I got up and walked down the beach, thinking about the war.

For Joss this was more of a victory than any killer app or IPO could ever be. This was what everything had been for—the artifice of wealth was only there to position him to win the game. And that game was afoot.

But I had never seen him more on edge than when he finally got what he wanted. He was like a girl getting ready for prom, every time he had a date with Maisey. Asking me over just to help him pick out shirts or ties or shoes. Everything had to be perfect, everything had to be ornamental, every little detail—every date a blockbuster production.

"Don't you get it?" I wanted to say. "You won. You don't have to pretend anymore."

It made me wonder whether he had won, or whether he had lost himself, somewhere along those billion steps that he took to get here.

```
<="<TITLE>"a>
// ------------------------------------------------
----------------------------
//   removeObjectFromChildren:obj
//
//   Recursive method which searches children and
children of all sub-nodes
//   to remove the given object.
// ------------------------------------------------
----------------------------
     -      (void)removeObjectFromChildren:(id)obj
     -      ---------------------------------------------
// <stuck);

"<here>"
```

Geezer was holding his breath, cheeks puffed out. Klondike was standing on his seat looking down at the keyboard, biting his fingernails. Joss was sitting in a chair about to press a button that would take Remake live.

It was November 5th. Guy Fawkes Day. Klondike's idea, naturally. Klondike looked at what they were doing as a revolution of sorts. Sticking it to the man. Makes sense, given that *V for Vendetta* gets a lot of airplay in Klondike's head. Joss didn't point out that it was hoping to stick it to the man by *becoming* the man. It didn't seem quite fair to Klondike.

The inside of the crumbling loft where they had been working nonstop for the last eighteen months had been painted chalkboard black so that they could scribble lines of code and notes and ideas and dirty pictures. By now it looked like the secret cave of a lost alien society. Impossible hieroglyphics. The living room and the bedroom with the two perpetually unmade beds, and even the bathroom and kitchenette, were filled with chalky scratches all over their walls; you couldn't even tell where one set of notes ended and the others began. You couldn't, that is, unless you were one of the loft's three tenants.

Either way, both Geezer and Klondike were all in, right from the beginning. Both ultimately doubting the idea would work out or whether it would work out well, of course, but both agreeing if Joss saw this as the only way to get past what he was going through, they would do what they could to help. And despite their razor edge philosophies and hacker morals, that's what they did.

Joss looked over at Geezer and then up at Klondike. "Ready?"

"No," they said in unison.

"Good," Joss remarked, and clicked PUBLISH.

Joss, Klondike and Geezer officially shared the same brain now. It had been an average of 10 hours of combined sleep every day between the three of them. And even when they slept they dreamt about code. Geezer had told Joss they heard him muttering in his sleep, "*a href=*, *a href=*," over and over like a blinking cursor. *a href=* is the first command of any line of HTML code that's going to the web. The primordial code, if you will, the line that made the whole of the Internet possible. It's basically like saying, "go here." Joss had probably typed it a hundred thousand times over the last year. And along with each of those lines he had embedded a message to Maisey. One line at a time.

Weeks were spent trying to get the Remake video reader right. In order to effectively insert someone into a video or movie or whatever, Remake needed to capture enough data about someone's face so that it could meld the user's facial features onto whoever they wanted to be melded onto. They set up a program function that would use the video capture of someone's laptop, phone or whatever--even the cheapest gadgets had video capabilities by now--and the Remake reader would take advantage of this. It would pop up and take the user through a series of prompts that pinpointed a person's facial features and movements. First they'd have to smile, talk, cry, laugh and whatever else the video capture software asked them to do, all while staying in the frame that they saw on their screen. After this was done the program would throw that data over to the video they were trying to insert themselves into and: voila.

It sounds simple enough, but it was a challenge to create something anyone could use on almost any device they had.

Joss, Geezer and Klondike were of course using themselves as the guinea pigs and each chose a music video, a movie and a TV show as the test cases. Klondike predictably picked *V for Vendetta*, morphing the mask that the main character wears into a facsimile of his own face.

"This won't work!" Geezer protested. "What is the bloody point of using a mask when the intention is to morph someone's soddin' face onto another person's soddin' face!"

But after a few weeks of trial and error, they had to admit that it did end up being pretty cool. Even if it didn't exactly prove what they were trying to prove. It proved something else. Which was just as good.

After they got that right they switched to *The Big Lebowski*, to unanimously positive results. Geezer picked *Dr. Who* as his test case and it worked swimmingly. Plus, seeing a black Dr. Who made the group realize that there would be some seriously racially charged uses for Remake, if this thing became as big as they hoped. All of them agreed that kind of controversy would be a good thing.

Joss decided to insert himself into a Lana Del Rey video. He wouldn't admit it, but he had developed a slight crush on the singer as they listened to her album on repeat the first few months of the project. Her lyrics seemed to him to be part-parody and part-homage to the lifestyles of the rich and brainless. Kinda similar to his other favorite artist: Kanye West. Joss inserted himself into a series of her videos, morphing his own face onto the tattooed lover she gets down with the whole time. Both Geezer and Klondike suggested that it would make excellent wanking material for him for years to come.

Once they got the technical part more or less down they had to move on to creating the design--they wanted it as user-friendly as possible. From then on out, it was mostly coding. Months and months and months of coding. They didn't have teams of foreign coders to help like the big boys did. Joss annihilated his keyboard, melting the letters and numbers off the plastic keys within the first few weeks. Geezer and Klondike never even had any letters or numbers on their keyboard to begin with. They were virtuosos and long ago found they could actually type faster going blind.

They had all been on a savage tear through a jungle of ones and zeroes, swinging from vine to vine, tumbling to the ground, picking themselves back up; you couldn't stop or the jungle would catch up and then you were done for. After the first few months everything became automatic. The digital world had completely subsumed their life.

"The three of us, we have stretched the bounds of human capacity and are now exploring its elastic atmosphere," Geezer said one afternoon in a post-sprint haze. Klondike and Joss just looked at each other. They were all losing it.

But now it was over. Or it was just beginning. It was impossible to say.

They had finally released it. With one stroke of a key they had sent Remake out to the masses who they hoped were eagerly sitting by their computers ready to swallow their creation whole.

"I don't hear any bombs dropping?" Klondike said, his hand to his ear.

"They're silent bombs," Geezer assured.

"I hope they're not too silent," Joss remarked anxiously.

They needed to make a splash. Gain attention. This first part of the plan was gonna be pretty hard to pull off--especially if they had a bunch of imitators in the mix before they could corner the market. Joss told me Geezer buried the code as far down as he could, which went against everything a true hacker usually stood for. But even then, some hired gun or hacker activist with a decent set of digits was bound to find the trick sooner or later, the part of the code that mattered, that was disguised as something else, behind several locked doors, in a maze, down a gutter buried under ten thousand miles of concrete. It was just the nature of programs and apps. The secret sauce would eventually be found.

"You have the metrics working?" Joss asked Klondike nervously.

"The metrics work better than the app," Klondike said defensively, still standing on the chair.

"What's the benchmark again?" Joss asked, even though he already knew. He just wanted to hear it out loud, as if he were Captain Kirk on the bridge of the Enterprise asking Scotty for a status update on the main power thrusters.

"There is more than one bloody index as you very well sodding know," Klondike snapped, inadvertently giving his best Scotty impersonation.

"I know, I know…" Joss put his hands up in surrender.

Klondike deflated at the last moment. "But," he rolled his eyes, "The leading indicator is this." Klondike pointed down to a screen on the left. "The Mass Index. If we can maintain a steady flow above 30 on this, we're solid fucking gold."

The way it worked was this: they gave access to about a thousand people and gave each of them 10 invites. Each of those invites got ten invites. And so on. If everything went even semi-smooth, then Remake could go viral, and sink its teeth firmly into the market before the copycats started appearing. They needed to stay above 30 on Klondike's Mass Index for at least nine months. If they could do that they could start shopping their app out. If not, they would pretty much bite the dust.

Joss was already down to forty-eight thousand in the Brogan Landing Fund and twenty of that was for bare essential marketing. If this didn't work, it was done. Game over. "Will you wake me up in nine months?" Joss asked.

"No problem, mate," Geezer slapped his back. "I got this here alarm on my phone. I'll nod off too and wake you up myself. We'll leave old K-Dike here to mind the store for half a year."

"I should be so lucky," Klondike grunted.

$$$

The first three months were brilliant. The Mass Index hovered around 35. They were elated. Then around the beginning of March people just stopped coming. The index took a nosedive. In May, it bottomed out at 15.

"I can't take it anymore," Joss said, letting his head fall down into his hands. "Pull the plug."

It was June 1st. Rent was due. Electric was due. Everything was due.

$5,455 left in the account after a runaway marketing campaign that, according to Klondike's metric system, had done worse than if they hadn't run it at all. "This is the kind of thing that would have taken off right away, if it was going to at all," Joss said breathlessly. "We're fooling ourselves and we have nothing left. Let's walk while we still have enough money to get you guys back home."

"You're irrational, man," Geezer pleaded.

Joss knew Geezer was right. But Joss had been irrational for the past eighteen months. And he was waking up to it all now. He was unraveling the bandages that had been wrapped around his eyes, the blinders that had allowed him to move forward at inhuman velocity. It was all crashing down before him. All the emotions that had led him to this impossible venture: the lust, the ambition, the greed. The gall that he alone would be worthy of asking for anything close to what he was asking. Joss sunk to a low, low place. Defeat. Utter defeat. A taste so bitter it would leave a hint of itself behind forever.

"Seriously, I'm going back to my house," Joss said wearily. "My parent's house," he corrected. "I should get used to saying that."

"Uh…" Klondike muttered.

Geezer sat on the table with his feet on a chair; his midnight eyes cautiously appraised Joss. Joss turned and looked at Klondike, who didn't usually make monosyllabic sounds. At least not when Joss was around.

"Uh…" Klondike repeated as he tapped away at his keyboard. "This couldn't… I mean, we have to wait." He wasn't so much talking to them as to himself. "I'm gonna send a copy of this log file to a few blokes," he continued, feverishly clacking away at his keys.

"What are you on about then?" Geezer asked skeptically, turning to look at the screen. Klondike's monitor was filled with a bunch of numbers clumped together then charted out in a way only Klondike could understand.

The whole system was one of Klondike's own inventions. He wrote the program but had a few colleagues with whom he shared the data. The colleagues were high enough up that Klondike couldn't even tell Geezer or Joss their names.

Geezer and Joss huddled around K's screen, pretending to take in the sea of data and make something meaningful out of it.

"Piss off!" Klondike said sharply. "I need room." He stared at the screen, in perplexed astonishment. "This... this just doesn't make any bloody sense." Klondike clacked away at his keys for a minute and then looked up at Joss. He gestured toward a laptop. "Go to Twitter and search #remake."

Joss opened his laptop, popped up the browser and clicked the shortcut on the menu bar. Before Joss even typed #remake into the Twitter search bar, his eyes caught the list that appeared below it. He turned silent and still.

"Well," Klondike said impatiently.

Joss didn't even register his voice. He just stared, as if he were seeing a ghost hover over the screen.

"Bloody hell, man." Klondike turned to look at him. "What do you have, then?"

"Joss?" Geezer looked at him concerned.

"We're trending," Joss whispered.

"We're a bloody fucking trending topic on Twitter?" Klondike bolted to his feet like Dr. Frankenstein.

"No," Joss said, correcting himself.

Klondike wilted, falling back into his seat.

"Come on, Joss," Geezer rasped in a hoarse, disappointed voice.

"We're not *a* trending topic." Joss looked up at them, a smile just beginning to break. "We are *all* the trending topics."

There was a silence that came over the room, one that's usually reserved for churches or monasteries.

"The whole fucking top ten." Joss felt drunk.

"Has that ever happened?" Geezer asked in a high and excited voice.

"I've never bloody heard of it," Klondike shook his head. "But that's why I had Joss check." He stared back at the feed of numbers cycling down his screen. "We're showing off the chart numbers on the indices. Every one is maxed out and it'll take me a day or two to recalibrate..."

"*But?*" Geezer asked impatiently.

Klondike's eyes were swimming in his head. "It can't be as high as it says. But there's certainly something big. But there's just too much traffic to make any sense of... whatever it is that's happening."

"Let's file that under nice-problem-to-have," Joss said, the smile now taking up most of his face.

"Is there a way to trace the source?" Geezer asked.

"Yes," Klondike said, snapping back into consciousness. He clacked away and then looked up to trace down a list. "This shows the social tree," he said to us without looking up or stopping. "There," he pointed to a list. "Here is the original conversation where most of the initial hits derived from, or at least where they sprang from:

lanadelrey: @kanyewest what's up with @remake is that for realz? #pissinginmypants

kanyewest: @lanadelrey I just put you into that Metropolis movie as that robot bride of Frankenstein. Check it. #thisisyournewvideo #remakeisthebombestshitever

ladygaga: @kanyewest I just made @bieber one of the lollipop kids #sexualfantasy

bieber: @kanywest @lanadelrey well I just put the both of you into an animal porn vid. @bieber out! #baaaaahhhdromance.

kanyewest: @bieber why do you have animal porn?

lanadelrey: have fun boys. #remakeyourself

Those three Twitter accounts alone had over one hundred million followers between them. Ten million of those people downloaded Remake over a period of 24 hours.

Then came the press circuit, which made Remake their top story that week, despite the civil unrest in Cleveland and a congressional hearing on war crimes occurring on Capital Hill. The electric daisy chain exploded. By the end of the week, Remake had been downloaded one hundred million times.

"Are you glad I talked you into that expensive server farm," Geezer demanded, gloating about what had been their biggest spend in the whole enterprise. Even Geezer had begun to

100

worry that he had single-handedly blown their chances by investing so heavily in it. But, because of his foresight, every one of the one hundred million new users was able to download Remake without the servers crashing.

Klondike and Joss looked at him and then at each other. On cue, they all started laughing hysterically and uncontrollably. They laughed so hard it turned into crying. When it was all done they just sat, stunned, and watched the sun come up from the roof of their building.

"Here's to bloody fucking capitalism," Klondike shouted across the rooftops of Reseda, raising a nearly empty bottle of Tanqueray. "May she allow us to dine on her," he pulled Joss in with his meaty arms, "until we decide to devour her!"

Joss looked back to the east as the sun came up over the San Bernardino Mountains, then to the west, toward that point on the horizon where his gaze had been fixed all this time. It occurred to him that he was probably going to beat the sun there, just as he had planned.

CHAPTER ELEVEN

Maisey, in stark contrast to Joss' heightened state of concern, was cool as a cucumber about the whole affair. Over those first set of weeks when things started coming together I got the feeling she didn't even think it was really happening, this re-alignment of star-crossed lovers. She had the carefree aplomb of someone who was walking through a dream. Maisey sailed through the calm, clear waters of June and past the fireworks of July. Settling in so well to her dual role as dutiful wife and illicit lover that I thought she'd be perfectly content to live this way forever.

And then toward the end of July, Brogan Landing came to visit.

I only found out he was arriving that day, when Maisey invited me to dinner, acting as if it were just another random guest that was coming over.

"I don't know if I can be in the same room with him," I said, disgusted.

"Oh, Charlie Middle," she said politely dismissive. "He *is* my father and your uncle or cousin, or however that works. He's a monster, but only occasionally."

"Maisey, how can you act as if it's no big deal," I said, bewildered.

"Because it isn't a big deal," she demanded. "Not anymore. We live with our past, for better and worse. What happens, happens, and we must move on." She smiled pleadingly. "It would make it all so much more bearable if you were there, though." Her eyes effortlessly provoked a sense of duty; as if she were a higher-ranking officer in whatever war games we were all playing, and I a loyal foot soldier.

I stared at her in disbelief, finally giving in with a nod.

"Whatever would I do without you," she said in her singsong voice. "Never leave me. Never as in forever."

I arrived at the doorstep of the Graft house at around 7pm, a bottle of Bordeaux in hand, and an unshakable reticence in my heart. James escorted me into a sitting room, deeper in the house than I'd yet been. Maisey ran over like a schoolgirl drunk for the first time. "Here he is, Daddy!" she cheered. "Our Charlie Middle, direct from the Midwest!"

Brogan Landing was redder and plumper than I remembered him being, although it was a decade since I last saw him. "How ya been, old boy," he said with a puffy smile.

"Not as bad as I could have been?" I offered, biting my tongue.

There was a long hardy laugh, the kind where the person was ready to laugh anyway but you caught them by surprise and actually said something funny.

Maisey and I walked down the steps into the den and sat together on the oversized couch. There was a bearskin rug so big it must have been prehistoric, and there were enough golden statues to fill the Taj Mahal. A fire was going and Reed and Mr. Landing sat in opposite, rustic-looking chairs that probably cost more than a fleet of vehicles.

With my better-educated eyes I saw Maisey's father as a demon, disguised in sandy blond hair and pastel jacket. He clutched a glass filled with an amber liquid and I imagined it as a potion he must keep consuming to prevent from changing back into demon form.

"Reed was just telling me you're quite a rider," he said with a crooked smile, taking a sip from his glass. There was a little laughter from Reed at my expense but I shrugged it off. "But I hear you have other things than horseplay going on with your life." Landing eyed me over the rim of his glasses, boxing out Reed.

Reed looked slightly injured at the slight. "Well, I'm trying," I said, honestly.

"Of course you are, my boy," he added, nodding his head in approval. "Good things to come, Charlie Middle," he assured me. "Good things to come." Brogan Landing drank by the gallon but it had no visible effect. He was steady as a battleship, with senses like sonar. So much so that I felt the need to cloak my true feelings all night. The effort exhausted me and I didn't contribute much to the conversation after a few initial rounds of Q&A. Mostly I watched Maisey, the limp dance that she did with her father. She had the personality of a mirror when she was around him, reflecting and deflecting all night long. She hid, like a scared child. What a stark contrast, I considered, from the every day Maisey as I saw her with Joss.

Being party to the cowering of a lioness only deepened my barely guarded contempt for my not-so-distant relative, Brogan Landing. And Reed, for that matter. But my contempt for Reed had been as instant as they say true love is.

"And what have you been doing with *yourself*, Maisey?" he asked accusingly.

"Whatever I can," she bowed her head, shrinking even deeper into the couch. "The staff—they're more than adequate. But keeping everything together, even from a high level, is challenging at times."

"That it is, I'm sure," Landing said with a patronizing wink.

Toward the end of the night, Reed started in on his tired rhetoric about class distinction and the bastardization of

104

wealth. "It used to be that you didn't have to dig too deep to tell who a person was," he blathered. "You could see it by their property, their car, their clothes. It took a certain kind once to be able to live in Agave. Now, anyone can just storm these gates with a checkbook and buy their way in. It used to be that only a certain type of people had that money. People you recognized. You understand?"

I was beginning to feel ill and turned to Maisey for some help. But she had tuned out long ago, cocooning herself into a ball and letting the oversized couch swallow her up. Even Mr. Landing looked restless and bored with the conversation.

"It's like that Joss Stember, across the lake in West Agave." Reed continued, oblivious to the weight of the name.

My stomach fell to the floor. I tried with everything I had not to turn to Maisey.

"He thinks he can just buy everyone's respect," Reed foamed. "But respect isn't purchased. It's inherited."

If you weren't looking for it you might have missed Brogan Landing's reaction to the name, Joss Stember. And I don't know about Maisey, but I certainly saw the twitch and the smoldering of recognition that occurred in that brief second. I almost imagined Landing had a second set of eyes that were burning into her at that very moment. It was all too much to bear without saying anything. I found myself having to work so hard to keep it all in, that I began to swirl.

"I think I see your point rather clearly, son," Landing said to Reed, like a predator waking up for a midnight snack. "And while it may seem like a general problem." He paused, with a furtive glance toward Maisey. "It's actually quite specific."

"That's what I've been saying all along!" Reed babbled, clueless.

"I think I may be able to help, my boy," Landing stirred. He spoke in a low rumble. It reminded me of what the sky sounds like before a walloping Midwest storm. I wasn't able to catch Maisey's eyes but I imagined that she too sensed the unsettling weather forecast: storms approaching, take shelter.

$$$

"This isn't going to end well for anybody, Maisey," I pleaded. "You have to tell Joss, and figure out what you're gonna do about Reed and your father."

It was the next day and we were on our way to meet one of Maisey's childhood friends who just moved to the city. She had notions of setting me up with her. I was at the wheel of a BMW that probably cost more than I'd make in the next ten years. I tried to gauge the level of concern on her face without taking my eyes off the road.

"For a romantic you sure think a lot, Charlie Middle." Her voice was far more carefree than appropriate, given the situation.

"Who ever said I was a romantic?" I asked in a high-pitched squeak.

"You may fool yourself," she drawled. "But you don't fool me."

"I'm worried, Maisey." I changed lanes to get out from behind a garbage truck spewing diesel fumes. "You're the one who was freaked out about me even telling Joss what really happened with your father and all that. This is ten times more dangerous. Aren't you the least bit concerned?"

"If I was concerned about everything my father could do or might do, I wouldn't be able to leave the house."

"What if he does something to Joss, though?" I begged. "He obviously suspects something, and you heard what he said to Reed, 'I think I may be able to help.' What could that mean?"

"While my father is ruthless, never more so than with his family, it is unlikely that he will do much to help Reed. He can't stand him and rarely visits because of that," she gave a little laugh. "It is only in matters where his own image or reputation or desires are at stake that he even bothers to get his hands dirty."

"And you don't think this qualifies?" I asked rhetorically. "He got you into this marriage for a reason right? To keep up appearances, or to build a better empire or something? Well, if you end up divorcing and running off with Joss how's that gonna look?"

"We are getting a little ahead of ourselves now, aren't we?" She tried to talk me down. "Why ruin something that's working so perfectly well?"

"What? Don't you understand what Joss' plans are? Do you think he wants to share you with Reed?"

"I am not a snack to be passed around," Maisey snapped. "Why must I always be at the whim of someone else's plans?"

"I didn't mean it like that, Maisey," I took a breath and apologized. "I just..."

"Oh Charlie Middle, I didn't mean to bark at you. It's just that I don't see the need to make any sudden moves just yet. Especially, as you say, if we are under any kind of scrutiny from my father."

"Yeah," I said, unsure how to proceed. "I just... I don't want you to get hurt. Or Joss."

"I was already dealt a fatal blow. Long ago," she said. "Until now, I hadn't considered the fact that there was anything still alive inside this shell that you see before you. I wasn't aware that I could hurt anymore, or love. You'll forgive me, if I don't want to veer too far in any direction just yet. This sweet spot I've seemed to luck into is a good deal more appealing than where I've been for the last four years. And I fear that if I venture away I may not be able to find it again. You can understand that, can't you?"

She offered me her hand and I took it in mine, keeping one on the wheel.

"Can't we just keep going," she asked. "We could drive and leave them all behind. Let them have their sick, twisted little games. We could just drive, Charlie Middle, you and me. All the way to Alaska or the North Pole. We can dress in white and they'll never find us," she trailed off and lost herself in an endless gaze out the window.

"From such great heights, come the biggest falls," she said absently. "From such great heights, come the biggest falls." As if it were the lyric to a nursery rhyme she had only just remembered.

```
// ----------------------------------------
----------------------------
NSImageView *fileIcon;
    NSTextField *fileName; I
    NSTextField *fileSize; built
    NSTextField *modDate; a weapon
    NSTextField *creationDate; to
    NSTextField *fileKindString; say
    NSURL *url; "<I love you
NSTextField *fileKindString;
    NSURL *url; "mute"
// ----------------------------------------
----------------------------
```

"**T**here are only three things you have to look out for, boys."
Harris Fink was behind the wheel of an eighteen-wheeler that
he'd "borrowed" from the shipping dock of one of the
companies he co-founded. "Problem is, no one knows what
they are." He held a cigar-sized joint in his left hand, blowing
smoke rings in the shape of dollar signs.

This was the final meeting that Joss, Geezer and Klondike were
taking. But they already knew who they were going with:
Bryan Jones, the rock star turned tech pioneer. He'd built his
empire with a file-sharing mentality. And he withstood the
blistering paces that Geezer and Klondike had been setting for
all the fat cats, waiting in line to pay them each a billion dollars
for a minority stake in Remake.

But Harris Fink requested to be the last person they talked to
and the three of them agreed. If only for the sheer spectacle of
it all.

"They can tell you what worked for them." Fink kept offering
Geezer and Joss the joint even though they had passed on it a
dozen times. "But they can't tell you what will work for *you*."

"Truth!" Klondike sounded like a member of the congregation.

He was matching Harris Fink blow for blow, unfazed by the fact that they were all barreling down the Hollywood freeway in a semi with a driver who was probably clinically insane and most definitely stoned out of his gourd.

Harris Albert Fink, 27, was a grizzled old-timer by then, having founded three of the fastest growing companies in Silicon Valley. But that doesn't mean he grew up. Harris was summarily fired from each of the three companies within a year, and several others in the intervening time. But despite his inability to hold a job the hackers and the suits kept coming back to him to put these massive deals together. Each time he was the glue that made it happen, as much as all the companies involved hated to admit it. Especially after he'd get busted, for example, wearing a Bin Laden mask and the company hat after a drug-fueled police chase through downtown Dubai.

Joss couldn't help but fall for him though. The first words out of Harris Fink's mouth were, "Remake is the karaoke of our generation." And even though they were going with Jones, Joss knew that Fink got it. Like no one had gotten it. Like even he hadn't gotten it. Harris was spouting sermons like he was on the mount. And continued to impress both Geezer and Klondike when he told a story of kidnapping his partner Danny Gluten, the founder of SoftCore, during negotiations with a buy-out firm. Just so Gluten wouldn't cave on a minor point.

At this point though, Joss and Geezer were wondering if this death trip down the 101 Freeway was one of Harris' tactics to get them to sign with him or whether he really had finally broke. They considered calling 911, but decided that would only push him further. Getting in a police chase was probably on Harris' bucket list.

"Harris," Joss cut in from the back seat, during one of Fink's infrequent lulls. "Just meeting you is worth the price of admission, man. We mean that sincerely. And this is certainly a once in a lifetime experience." Joss gripped the oh-shit bar as Harris swerved into the next lane almost taking out a suburban. "But..."

"Yeah I know," Harris interrupted. "You're going with Jones." He looked at Joss in the rearview mirror, an evil grin on his face, as if he were in on a joke Joss wasn't. "We can just skip the bullshit, boys," Fink nodded respectfully. "I haven't seen anyone with your morals this close to Silicon Valley since... oh wait. NEVER."

Klondike laughed which started him into a coughing jag.

"So I'm not gonna bullshit with you. And to save time," Harris continued. "Maybe you'd return the favor."

Joss, Geezer and Klondike just nodded, uneager to press the manic mogul while he still had their lives in his hands. Literally.

"When you're in his presence," Joss remarked to me once, "there's the persistent but not entirely uncomfortable notion that you're under his control." It was one of the many reasons that Joss infrequently socialized with Harris.

"Brogan Landing." Harris said the name as if it were a venereal disease. He looked around to Geezer and Klondike, and then at Joss. "He has never been too kind to my operation." He took a puff off the Havana blunt he still had going. "I'm dirty." He looked at them. "There, I said it. And you know what that makes me, boys?"

They didn't make a sound.

"The most honest man in Silicon Valley." He downshifted and cut across three lanes nearly sideswiping a minivan full of kids. "Brogan Landing decided he didn't like me, from the moment we met. Maybe it had something to do with me ogling his daughter. Anyway, he had me blackballed at most of the institutions in the Valley when I was starting out." Harris grunted as if reliving the memory. "But that didn't stop me from making deals. It just made other people richer instead of the ones that blackballed me. That pissed him off good. So he's had it in for me since."

"So you want revenge? I don't understand," Joss interjected.

"Yeah, what's this all about, then," Geezer added.

"This shit's bloody brilliant, man," Klondike remarked, holding up the blunt with a lazy grin plastered on his face.

"You're mental," Geezer shouted at Klondike.

Harris continued. "Several weeks ago my colleagues and I got wind that there was a potential big-buy coming through. Brogan Landing was shopping for a firm to create a trick IPO buy-out. It's this weird loophole congress just created out of an appropriations bill. It basically lets a certain type of investor buy back enough shares during the IPO to effectively take over the company from its owners. A sham, really."

Geezer and Joss turned to each other in confusion.

"Was that us?" Klondike asked nervously.

Geezer and Joss turned to Klondike and then back to Harris. Apparently Klondike wasn't too stoned to read between the lines.

"Yes," Fink beamed, haloed by a cloud of smoke. "It is indeed you. We got word of it and thought, there must be something else here. We dug a little deeper and let's just say you and Brogan Landing," Harris looked at Joss in the rearview, "must have issues."

Joss looked back at him, blankly.

"I don't know, man," Geezer whispered to Joss a little louder than he had intended. "He could be playing us for one. We have to consider what he has to gain."

"Exactly," Harris agreed unperturbed. "What do I have to gain? Maybe I make a hundred million off of you?" He looked at the three of them with a piteous expression. "I mean, come on let's face it, guys. You got a fad that could be replicated by a team of Malaysians for the cost of a few bowls of rice. And I shit ten million dollars worth of caviar a year." He took a long drag off his stogie and let out a wide, almost anatomical trail of smoke. "But every single one of those people you talked to about putting up cash, has a million percent more vested interest in Brogan Landing than in your broke asses. Including your precious Bryan fucking Jones."

Geezer, Joss and Klondike stared at each other.

"You mean nothing to them," Harris continued. "A video game vs. a media empire? Fuggedaboutit. Even if you take him to court, he'll have you tied up in the wind so long you'll be nothing but a dried-out sock by the time you're finished. And he'll still be a titan." He passed the joint back to Klondike. "I'm not saying I'm the best game in town, boys." Harris turned to look Joss square in the eyes. "I'm saying I'm the only game in town."

$$$

Murder, murder in black convertibles
I kill a block

I murder avenues
I rape and pillage a village
Women and children
Everybody wanna know
What my Achilles heel is
LOVE
I don't get enough of it
All I get is these vampires and blood suckers
*All I see is these n****s I've made millionaires*
Milling about
Spilling there feelings in the air
*All I see is these fake f***s with no fangs*
Tryna draw blood from my ice-cold veins
(Sniff!) I smell a massacre (beat) (beat) (Gunshot)
Seems to be the only way to back you bastards the
*f*** up*

Joss was standing shoulder to shoulder with Harris, in downtown Paris, watching Jay-Z perform with Kanye at the official release party for Remake™. It would go public in two days with an initial IPO offering of twenty billion dollars. The four of them: Joss, Geezer, Klondike and Harris each received two billion dollar payouts and everyone but Harris retained a majority control that paid them much more than that. Joss thought to himself that the song they were singing onstage could have been the theme song to Harris' life.

Profit
Profit
*N**** I got it*
Everybody knows
*I'm a motherf***ing monster*

"I'm gonna watch out for you boys. For life." He gave them all a giant bear hug, "But you gotta go forward without me being part of the company."

Harris passed a joint the size of a baseball bat over to one of the members of Odd Future. It was post-concert and they were all in a suite that was so luxury it wasn't even listed as a room in the hotel. It took up the entire thirteenth floor. Joss tried to argue with Harris but he was coughing so hard he couldn't get any words out.

"Believe me, kid," Harris handed Joss a bottle of water. "You don't want me around past this point. It gets bad. I sort of self-destruct at some point. And unlike every other god-forsaken asshole in the Valley, I like you guys." He bore down on Joss. "Besides, you don't need any extra attention. You already got a bullseye on your back."

Joss thought about Landing. And thought of the rumors he had heard. How he fired a building full of lawyers and lobbyists when they failed to block the Remake IPO. Joss couldn't help but let a grin leak onto his face. The grin quickly subsided, though, as his thoughts moved to Maisey.

Joss laid back on the white couch of the high roller suite, stoned out of his mind. He felt the blood rush to his head and could hear someone talking to him. He looked up through blurred out eyes to see Thom Yorke extending his hand out for Joss to shake it. But Joss couldn't seem to make his body move. "You're my rock god," is all he managed. Thom Yorke just winced in disgust and walked away.

 "I've lost the plot," Joss said to Geezer the next morning, as they watched the sun come up from the roof of the hotel.

"What do you mean," Geezer asked, gently. "You've got the hard part done. You've pulled off the miracle."

"Don't you realize?" Joss pleaded. "I've come this far on the thought, the idea of her. I never thought I would actually get here. Now I'm not just faced with the *idea of her*, I have to deal with the *actual her*. And I'm not fucking ready to do that. I have no idea what I'm gonna say. I only get one chance and I'm terrified I'm going to blow it."

There was silence from Geezer, which was even more disturbing. He's usually always got the right words on hand. And even if they aren't the right ones they're close enough. But Geezer wasn't making a sound; he was just looking at Joss as if he had to be careful what he said. Or Joss might just blow.

KID BILLIONAIRE BAILS BUT IS HE GONE FOR GOOD?

Los Angeles, CA – Joss Stember was reported missing last April. Not by his family or friends, but by the media. Every news media outlet, every reporter and every paparazzi photographer were all asking the same question: Where in the World is Joss Stember?

After several months of globe-hopping parties with the likes of Jay-Z, Lady Gaga and former President Bill Clinton, and too-numerous-to-count romantic ties, Joss Stember shocked the tech world and Wall Street alike when he sold his remaining interest in his company, Remake™, and announced he would be taking an extended retreat to an undisclosed location.

Mr. Stember, the nineteen-year-old billionaire, sent thanks and well-wishes out to all of the people who had helped support what he was doing. While family and friends remained tight-lipped, unnamed sources have pinned his current location to such far-flung places as New Zealand, the North Pole, the Netherlands and Nepal. One inside source even claimed he had changed his identity altogether, and is now a six-foot blonde female.

It's been nine months now, and the media uproar has died down from its initial fever pitch. But everyone still seems to be asking the same question to themselves: where in the world is Joss Stember? And when will he return? — *Carol Barnes, Features Editor, Gossip Hourly*

CHAPTER THIRTEEN

"Oh yeah," I said to Joss. "I'm supposed to invite you over for early supper tomorrow—Reed's invitation."

It was mid-August and the nights were unseasonably warm for Northern California, or so I was told. In the Midwest you didn't go outside in August without your clothes sticking to your body like Saran Wrap. So this was nothing to m. I could take the heat. Or at least I though I could.

"Wouldn't that just be so cozy?" I added. "You, Maisey, Reed and I? Can't you imagine all the fun things we'd have to talk about?"

"What time?" he asked, unblinking, sitting on a high stone chair in a cavernous room dedicated to pre-feudal Japan.

"What time?" I responded with a shallow laugh. "How about never."

"Why?" He asked without a hint of irony.

"Are we even having this conversation?" I pleaded. "It's totally a trap."

"If we know it's a trap," he smiled, "then how can it be a trap?"

I tried to follow the logic. "Unless *that's* the trap," I parried.

"I'm going," Joss said. "Tell them I'll be there."

I shook my head. "No friggin' way."

"Tell them I'll be there," he said soberly, "or else I'll go over there and tell them myself. I'll end it all right now." There was a
118

flash of something nearly sinister in his eyes, just the barest twinkle; but he remained cool and composed, as always.

His threat actually stirred something in me, but it wasn't worry for him or Maisey. It was the realization that if it all ended, *where would I be?* This war, or whatever you want to call it, had become the primary function of my existence. So much so that I realized I didn't really want it to end, sick as that sounded. I didn't want to see anyone hurt in the process and I wanted Joss to get the girl. I just... didn't want it to end. Not yet.

$$$

"I have no idea what Reed is up to," Maisey paced back and forth, lighting another cigarette before laying back down on her chaise lounge. "But he's definitely up to something."

"That's what I was trying to tell Joss," I said, relieved that clearer heads were beginning to prevail. "He has it in his head that he's coming—hell or high water."

A mischievous smile escaped her lips before she was able to pull it back "Is that so?" She had a playful drawl. "A brash young man, that Joss Stember. Wouldn't you say? Brash?"

"Far too much so for my taste," I said, trying to display my concern for him and her both.

She looked almost wounded as I got up from the deck chair and walked over to the side of the pool, bending down to dip my fingers in the water. "I think your heater's broken," I said without turning back to her. "The pool's boiling hot."

"That's not the pool; it's the Jacuzzi," she corrected me.

While it was round like a Jacuzzi, it was unmistakably a rather large pool. The sun became obscured by an unseasonal set of bruised clouds that passed slowly overhead like an alien invasion. "Just because you change what you call things doesn't mean they change what they are," I said to her.

There was no response, just the subtle wind along the back of my neck and the sound of a billion blades of grass clapping their hands, hoping to bring the sun back out for an encore.

$$$

"So you and Maisey knew each other as kids," Reed asked Joss, taking sips of his vodka tonic between pauses.

Most of Reed's questions were phrased as statements.

We sat at a white linen table in the Graft's solarium—its doors and windows opened letting the early-evening breezes make their way around the room like curious guests.

Joss shifted in his chair. "Well, it was brief," he responded, putting on his sunglasses and taking them off again. "We ran in different circles." Joss glanced at Maisey who pretended to be sunbathing in the corner of the glass room. The last of the direct sun was leaking through like a spotlight.

"Oh," Reed followed up. "And what circles were those?"

This was a mistake, I kept saying to myself. As if just by saying it I could trace our steps back and redirect them.

"You know," Joss said, swallowing his words. "Different sides of the tracks."

"Ahh, yes," Reed concurred as if connecting a previous thought, "the proverbial tracks." There was a slight pause as he took another hit off his drink. "So how then did you manage to cross those tracks? That is, how did you end up on Maisey's side?"

I was thinking I'd almost rather have had Reed launch directly into one of his diatribes about how the classes should be segregated to insure proper breeding, instead of pacing around the subject trying to draw Joss into this bullshit game.

"Luck," Joss stared back at Reed, taking the challenge.

"I hear the Pettigrews are planning to move again," Maisey remarked to Reed, as if it were the most interesting development since the electric light bulb.

"They're a tiresome lot," Reed seemed to agree as if there was an entire subtext to the Pettigrews decision—one that only Maisey and him seemed to be privy to.

"Who was it that brought Redo public?" Reed turned his focus back on Joss, during a lull in our attempts to keep their conversation at bay.

Joss held steady. "You mean Remake. It was Ludlow/Massey."

"A less prestigious firm," Reed raised his eyebrows. "How did you get in touch with them?"

Maisey and I exchanged nervous glances, not knowing where the conversation was going.

"Harris Fink," Joss said flatly, glancing sideways.

"The drug addict," Reed said with modest delight. "Okay, I remember hearing about that now that you mention it. Unfortunate the way it all turned out for him." Reed gave a knowing glance to Joss. "I hear they have yet to uncover most of the illicit transactions and shady dealings. Word is they spread wide and far."

"Harris is doing just fine," Joss assured Reed. "And I am out of the business. Retired," he added with a tight nod.

"Yes. Not everyone's cracked up for it." Reed took a hit off his Vodka Tonic. "So much pressure. It's almost unfair for those who lack those innate social tendencies that others are simply born with. Some things just can't be learned."

"I had other things to focus on."

"I detest the cold feeling of this room," Maisey chirped. "Reed, don't you think we should do something to make it more intimate?" The air was breathing heavily. "Reed?" Maisey begged.

Joss looked at Maisey, who wouldn't make eye contact with him. After a moment of calculation, he took the napkin from his lap and placed it next to his untouched gold-flaked truffle mousse. "If you'll excuse me," he turned to Reed and then back to Maisey. "I think I should be going."

"What on Earth for," Reed chuckled in a mocking tone.

"I've exhausted my appetite," Joss answered, turning to meet Reed's bilious gaze.

"I hardly believe that to be true," Reed's grey eyes darted back and forth between Joss and Maisey. "Your appetite strikes me as insatiable."

I braced myself for an impending collision.

"Why don't we put ourselves all in," Reed challenged.

"A game of cards then?" I interjected.

"No," Reed answered without even looking at me. "I've invited you here, Mr. Stember. And it wasn't to point fingers. It was to get the cut of your jib. But I realize now that this is not the way to do that."

"Reed, just let him go," Maisey complained.

"No, I don't think I will, dear." Reed turned to Joss. "I've got invitations to a party happening in the city tonight, not just a normal one, mind you." He got up from his chair. "It's an underground event to kick off a very exciting venture. It starts at midnight and lasts for 24 hours. They're trying to bring bacchanalia back. It's dangerous and reckless and out of control. Something, Mr. Stember, that I would assume is right up your alley."

"I don't think so."

"Think?" Reed said with a challenging gaze. "Is that really what we've come to now? Can't we just set caution aside for once," he mocked. "We're all adults here, aren't we?"

No, I thought to myself. We are not.

"Reed," Maisey said impatiently. "That's enough. It's been a long night already and it's barely dark."

"Nonsense." Reed clapped his hands and a uniformed girl scuttled from out of a dark recess with four champagne glasses on a silver tray. "The night hasn't even begun, my precious love."

After we all had a drink in our hands Reed stood up. "To new adventures, *with old friends*." He smiled and raised his glass.

We all drank. The only thing left to do, really.

"This champagne was given to my father by the Rothschild's. It's said to be over two centuries old." Reed nodded his head as if accepting a compliment. "I thought this might be a nice way to start our engines, if you will."

"I think our engines are already in overdrive," Maisey quipped.

"Yes," Reed looked at her with barely hidden scorn. "Some of us are running a little hot."

James made his way into the room and over to Reed, who whispered something in James' ear.

"Reed, I have work in the morning," I interjected, trying with my whole might to avoid what seemed to be a showdown of wills.

"Oh, please, Charlie," Reed almost spit. "I'll call in sick for you. God forbid a TPS report doesn't get filed. Aren't you the one who said we needed more fun, more parties?"

"I don't think so--"

"Hey, Charlie," he interrupted. "You're coming to the party."

There wasn't much I could say.

"Dear," Reed said, looking at Joss but addressing Maisey. "Why don't you drive with Mr. Stember? The two of you can catch up on *old times*." Reed gave a nod to Joss. "You can chat about the tracks and which side is which."

"What about Charlie?" Maisey said looking at me for help.

"Charlie will come with me. We'll take the Maybachs—make it a race. They're just hankering to be broken in." Reed turned his gaze toward Joss, who was wavering. "Is it too much for you, after all, Old Sport? I don't want to make you feel... out of place."

There was a tense moment of silence and anticipation. "No," Joss turned to Maisey, "I'd love the chance to catch up on old times."

124

Maisey turned to me, then to Reed. "If you want we could just have the both of you pull out your cocks right now, and get the ruler out," she said with a desperate, cutting stare.

"I've always said you knew how to take the true measure of a man," Reed said with an acid smile.

And before I could think of a way out of it, the four of us had been ushered out to the front drive. The two Aryan colored Mercedes Maybachs sat side by side, like an advertisement for excess. James was there, handing Reed both sets of keys.

"To the winner go the spoils." Reed tossed Joss a set of keys and let out an arch laugh as he slid into his driver seat.

Joss opened the door for Maisey and walked around to the other side.

"And what are the spoils?" Joss asked.

"Whatever you'll be able to do without!" Reed shouted over the revving engine.

And in a swirl of dust and gravel the race began.

```
// ----------------------------------------------
----------------------------
<home>" a>
// ----------------------------------------------
----------------------------
```

Joss had imagined himself escaping to a remote island off Greece, maybe even buying it in order to guarantee security. Land was cheap there, Harris had told him. Or maybe some cave in Northern India. He even considered Alaska or perhaps Tahiti. One of the Google guys had even offered his condo on Lunar One.

Joss scratched away at the surface of the problem so hard that he eventually saw his own reflection. It was then he realized exactly where he needed to go. Where he needed to be in order to think through what he was doing and for whom he was doing it.

"It's been nine months, dude." Anthony remarked, out of nowhere.

Joss looked up from his laptop, confused. "What?"

"You've been hiding out in this house for nine months," Anthony clarified. "You could have had a baby in that time." Anthony sat on Joss' bed.

"I could not have had a baby."

Joss was laid out on the floor of his old bedroom, in his parents' house. Feet draped up over the foot of the bed, laptop on his chest. Standard work-mode. Except that work had changed over the last set of months. No longer was he stringing together millions of lines of code in order to create a full functioning, cross-browser compatible application set.

No, now Joss was doing something much more complex and challenging: trying to figure out what the hell he was gonna say to Maisey. And no matter how hard he tried he just couldn't figure it out.

"I know if there was any woman in earshot I'd be struck with a mallet, but it actually does kind of feel like I'm having a baby." Joss rested his hand on his stomach. "I'm definitely carrying something inside of me. No doubt about that. And it doesn't want to come out, but it needs to. And no matter what I do I just can't get comfortable."

"My God," Anthony sat up in epiphany, looking at Joss.

"What," Joss said squinting his eyes suspiciously.

"Problem solved!" Anthony declared. "There's your icebreaker for Maisey: honey, I'm pregnant. And I think it's yours."

Their laughter quickly died.

"I'm sorry, Joss." Anthony looked embarrassed. "That was probably the wrong thing to say. I mean it definitely was the wrong thing."

"Dude, please," Joss threw an empty Cheetos bag at Anthony. "I know what you meant and it *was* funny. Even if it's also sad. The saddest things are the funniest."

Anthony sat up, locking his arms around his knees. "In all seriousness, man," he looked down soberly at Joss, "you've been sitting on that floor hiding out in here for nine months. That's at least eight months too long. You gotta shit or get off the pot, homey. This past life regression therapy isn't doing you any good. It's just delaying the inevitable."

"What's this tough love all of a sudden?" Joss smirked.

"It's just love, man. The tough part is already included in the package. And it isn't so *all of a sudden*, either. I've been on you for the last few months."

"Thanks, coach," Joss sighed. "That may sound good on paper. But failure isn't an option for me. My velocity is set for the heart of the sun and if something doesn't happen, that's exactly where I'll end up. Burnt to a crisp."

"It's not even cool to joke about that, man."

"Who said I'm joking?" Joss looked at Anthony and held his stare.

Anthony took a deep inhale and then let it out, shaking his head. "I love you, hermano." He got up off the bed and headed to the door. "But you are a fucking loco wannabe gringo who doesn't know what's good for him." Ducking under the chin-up bar, Anthony turned back to Joss, with a mixture of frustration and hurt in his eyes, and walked out without a word.

Joss stared at the ceiling as if it might have something to say. The shades were blowing shadows on the wall and there were starry drops of sunlight that danced on top of the shadows. It made the ceiling look like a summertime lake.

"Tiene razón," Joss thought. "He's right."

CHAPTER FIFTEEN

"**I** just want to say that this is not how I want to go out, Reed."

I was as close to death as I'd ever been. Granted, that'd not been all that many years and I've had few, if any, *real* brushes with death. But you never explore the depths of your existence more than when it's being threatened.

"I know I don't have the money to bribe you, man. Or the will to make you slow down. But just know that if I could I would give you a part of my soul if you'd just pull over."

"Did you say something, Charlie?" Reed looked at me with an evil set of eyes that knew exactly what I was saying.

He was clocking 135 MPH weaving in and out of cars going half that speed. There was something about his demeanor that had shifted a while ago, and he seemed like he was on something. *Power* by Kanye West was pumping so loud from the speakers that I could no longer distinguish my heartbeat from the bump of the bass. I clamped my eyes closed, preparing for impact, as a Hummer up ahead veered over into the lane we were rocketing though. A semi was taking the Hummer's place in the lane it vacated and there would be no human way possible to avoid the collision that was about to happen.

"I will tell Joss that I made you stop. Please, whatever it takes…"

I peeled my eyes open expecting to see an exit ramp to the afterlife ahead of us. But somehow we were still traveling in one piece. I looked back through the rear window, sure I'd see the Hummer upturned or the semi jackknifed in our wake. But I couldn't even see evidence of either vehicle behind us anymore.

"Aren't you even worried about other people?" I begged. "You seem like a charitable person, Reed."

He got the joke, which was much more of a desperate plea than a joke, and started laughing even more maniacally. "God makes too much of a dividend off Legacy Partners to ever let anything happen to me, Charlie."

"That isn't God," I mumbled. But we were coming up quickly on a cluster of cars blocking each lane and Reed didn't appear to regard them at all. In fact, he sped up.

I couldn't even look at the speedometer anymore. I just counted my breaths, gripping the oh-shit bar on the dash so hard that not only will my fingerprints forever be accessible from it but there should be enough of my DNA left over to start a colony of Charlie Middles.

I hold onto the lyrics of the Kanye song, as if it were a lifeline keeping me tethered to this world.

> *"No one man should have all that power/the clock's ticking /I just count the hours/Stop trippin'/I'm trippin' off the power/21st Century Schizoid..."*

"I don't even think they're racing anymore, Reed." I made yet another plea for my life.

"I'm not racing *him*, Charlie," Reed turned to me with a look of disgust. I violently gestured for him to get his eyes back on the road ahead. "The only competition one truly has in this world is oneself."

At first I blinked, thinking I hadn't heard correctly. That was by far the deepest thought I'd ever heard from Reed. Hands-down the truest thing he'd ever said. It almost frightened me more than the thought of crashing.

130

"I wish it weren't true," he said with a wisp of sadness. "I wish there were still families that had the purity we Grafts have. But, sadly, the mongrels have beset the bloodlines of most of the world's elite."

I was almost relieved to know that Reed hadn't lost his hyper-delusional mindset. I'm not sure I could have stomached it if I actually found a sympathetic or solid core to his existence.

We exited the off ramp and I patted my body down to make sure I was still in it.

Reed chose to cruise smoothly through the city streets instead of keeping up the Formula One pace of the highway. "Text them to see how far behind they are," he ordered.

Half of my body was still traveling at 135MPH. The other half was passed out from the exhaustion of watching my life pass before me. It took a few minutes before my fingers would even register the signals coming from my brain.

"We're in the city," I messaged Maisey. "What's your ETA?"

"Tell Reed to go ball a couple of hipster chicks," Maisey typed back. "We'll meet you at Zanzibar in an hour."

Reed let out a bitchy sigh when I told him the plans. "Well, why don't we go get coffee in the Mission," he suggested. "There's something about the way those girls keep themselves, like drunken, oversexed librarians." He made a u-turn without even looking. "It's intoxicating," he added, a disturbing arousal in his voice.

Maisey really had him pegged. We pulled up to a parking space in front of the Bump and Grind coffee house on Valencia after Reed nearly took out a couple cyclists. You could see the disappointment in his eyes when the young bikers averted the collision. "I almost got one last week," he said with a trace of regret in his voice. Regret that he didn't actually succeed. "A fucking taco truck got in the way at the last minute and I had to brake."

I took a calming breath, getting myself together, and prayed that I wouldn't have to be alone with Reed for very much longer.

There was a line out the door of the coffee house, but Reed walked through the crowd and up to the counter as if he owned the place. He laid two Benjamins on the counter and ordered two Fernet Lattes, declaring that everyone's drink was on him.

"I never wait in line," he grimaced. "And these primped up gutter rats are more than happy to accept a handout," he looked around scoping the place out.

He guided us to a table in the corner. "Well, we're all out in the open now, right?" He said as we slid into the booth. A girl in ballet tights and a fedora squeezed in and took a seat on Reed's lap. She whispered something into his ear and slid out again, then wound her way through the crowd and disappeared into a back room. "Excuse me a second, Charlie. I have to take care of some business." He dropped another hundred-dollar bill on the table. "That will buy you a half hour," he winked.

Reed slimed his way out of the booth and took up the trail of the girl in the fedora, disappearing into the same back room.

He sure doesn't disappoint, I reflected. Maisey did make it seem like he messed around on her, I guess I just thought maybe she was trying to justify her own actions. But the more time I spent with him the more I realized this trail of depravity was an endless road for Reed.

"You look young," a voice crept up behind me.

A nubile wisp of flesh with jet-black hair twisted around the booth and slid in next to me, eying the hundred-dollar bill. She was wearing a battered army jacket that appeared to be servicing as both top and bottom. Day-Glo fishnets clung to her skinny legs, which crept out the bottom of the jacket like stalks of corn that weren't even close to ripe yet. Black lipstick stood in contrast to her white, manga make-up. Two rounded orbs of turquoise blinked seductively, like impossibly large neon signs that screamed "Vacancy."

"Uh..." I stammered, taken off-guard. "Well, you look too young to even be called young."

She let out a tinkling laugh that sounded like wind chimes in a hurricane. "I may look young, but I act old."

I looked around at the Bump and Grind, so ultra modern hip, but slithering with illicit activity. A smorgasbord of depraved fantasies.

"Listen," I said feeling a bit queasy. "I'm just waiting on a friend," my throat tightened, protesting the use of the word *friend* in reference to Reed. "You're beautiful, I'm just not here for... you know."

A loud slap split through the din of wordless music and the caffeinated laughter of the nearby tables. "Fuck-off," the girl said as I registered that I was the one who had just been slapped. And then she laughed, as if it were the most hilarious joke ever. "I bet you like the rough stuff. All you Richies do."

I looked at her completely bewildered, lifting my hand to my cheek. "I most certainly do not like the rough stuff," I said, irritated and confused. "And I'm not a Richie," I added, as if that were the real slap in the face.

"Yeah right." She scrunched her face into a question mark. "Are you just his boy-toy or something?"

"No! I am not his *boytoy*," I assured her. "I'm not anyone's boytoy for that matter."

"Too bad," she said licking her lips. "You look like you'd be fun to play with."

She pretended to grab at the growing bulge between my legs and I swatted her hand away reflexively.

"Geez," she giggled.

Despite the fact that I wasn't completely recovered from the death mobile, and the girl looked like she was barely out of junior high, I was rather taken with her. In a perverted old man sort of way, I guess. I didn't want to be; I didn't want any part of Reed's dirty little playpen. "I'm old enough to be your... much older brother."

She sized me up closely. "Sweetie, I'm 21. I'm probably old enough to be your... *not much* older sister."

I stared at her suspiciously.

"I definitely undress to impress the pedo set," she said pulling out a thin wallet from somewhere under her jacket. "But I'm as legal as a right turn on a red." She showed me what at least looked like a valid license. It took me a second to believe that it was actually her in the photo, but the eyes were a dead giveaway. They looked electric even in the dulled-out DMV pic.

"Oh," I said, chastened, realizing she was three years my senior. "You could have fooled me."

"Something tells me I wouldn't be the first," she said in a lustful giggle. "I'm just kidding." She gave me a peck on the cheek. "You're super-cute."

134

"Oh," I said shyly. "Thank you."

"Oh my god, 'thank you?' What are you from the Midwest or something? You're fucking adorable." She put her hands on my cheeks and pulled me in close, and before I knew it her lips were pressed up softly against mine. My heart was sweating and a charge ran through my center; I melted into the seat as her lips parted mine and our tongues came together in a writhing embrace. It'd been so long I nearly let loose in my shorts before I could remember to breathe.

"What's your name?" I said, as if waking from a dream.

"Charlie," she answered. "Charlie Angel."

"What?"

"Too corny?" she laughed, somewhat self-consciously.

"No," I said desperately. "I just... *My* name is Charlie too," I tried to explain. "Charlie Middle," I added.

"Charlie-fucking-Middle," she demanded gleefully. "Of course."

I looked around self-consciously.

"My real name's Charlize. Charlize Hickenbottom," she smiled. "But don't tell anyone."

"Oh, so Charlie Angel is like a stage name?"

"It's not what you think," she tried to explain. "I'm not a prostitute or anything."

I put my hands up in defense.

"I do a bit of burlesque, but nothing too touchy feely. I just hang around and flirt. They don't expect us to... you know..." she gestured to a few other girls around the room, who also appeared to be dressed for some kind of techno carnival. "I mean, I don't do anything but flirt and maybe the occasional kiss. Some of the other girls like Candy are a bit more… *professional*. But that's strictly off the record." She looked around and caught the eye of some guy in the corner. "Listen, I should probably let you go."

I handed her the hundred-dollar bill that Reed had left and smiled nervously. She looked at me confused, and a little embarrassed. "No," I stammered, "I'm not trying to… I mean I know you're not a prostitute. But if I give you this, can you just sit with me?" I said gesturing towards the guy in the corner.

Her shoulders lowered and her body relaxed into mine. "Of course," she said, handing back the bill, "but you don't have to pay me."

"No," I demanded. "You keep that. It's not mine… I mean, I don't need it." I looked at her sparkling lips. "Please take it."

She eyed me with a mischievous grin. "I really have never done this… but do you want me to show you the back room?"

Her hands slid across my chest and I unconsciously said, "Yes, please." And then caught myself, "I mean, no. I don't want that from you." A hurt look leaked into her eyes. "No, I mean I *do* want that from you… I mean, I don't want it to be like that." I buried my head in my hands in defeat.

"Hey, sugar," she said, tracing her fingers along my cheek. "You're the sweetest thing ever." She nibbled on my ear and I felt my will go up in a puff of smoke. "I get off at 12:00, what are you up to?"

"Well…" I considered Maisey and Joss. "I'm supposed to meet some friends at a party." I looked at my watch. 10:05.

Reed appeared out of nowhere. "I see you decided to have a snack after all." He groped Charlize with his eyes and I nearly decked him.

"Charlize is a friend of mine," I warned him.

"Charlize and Charlie," he busted out laughing, and I glared at him. "Okay, okay, Charlie boy. Don't get your panties in a wad." He looked her up and down suspiciously and then looked at me. "I guess you've found your soul mate," he said, with barely disguised revulsion.

"She gets off at twelve, and I want to bring her with us."

Reed looked over at the man standing in the corner, the same one Charlize had eyed, and nodded in Charlize's direction, dropping another hundred on the table. The guy tipped his hat at Reed.

"I think we just got Charlize the rest of the night off," Reed said with a cocky grin. "Let's go. I have something to pick up before we meet the rest of the Donner party."

Charlize looked unsure about Reed, which instantly doubled my respect for her. But I gave her my best Midwestern puppy-dog eyes and she acquiesced. We passed a table full of wanna-be droogs and made our way out onto Valencia Street, which was teeming with fleet-footed hipsters and vendor carts soaked in bacon fat and migrant sweat.

We got to the car and Charlize hesitated, looking at me skeptically. I nodded, as if to say, "it's safe." But the truth is I wasn't so sure about that. Charlize wisely opted for the back seat and I took the front, silently willing Reed to be civil and not take out any cyclists or pedestrians. Just for tonight.

"Alrighty then." He hummed a few bars of Beethoven's fifth and the Maybach's engines revved on. "The next act begins." We sped out of the Mission and made our way toward the glistening bustle of downtown.

CHAPTER SIXTEEN

```
// --------------------------------------------------
---------------------------
<integration proceeding>"
<migration complete>
```

"It's on!" Harris Fink's text came through on Joss' mobile.

"Harris. Don't fuck with me," Joss texted back.

"I *told them* you were the genuine article. I guess I can't fault them for not taking *my* word for it. But you absolutely killed it last weekend. They said your visit was the capper."

"No shit?" Joss typed and took a deep breath, smiling from ear to ear.

"Well... we both know what the real capper was."

Landing, Joss smiled to himself.

It just so happens that the heirs of Linus Apple, a sister and brother, were taken to court by Brogan Landing over estate matters. It left a bad taste in their mouths, as did Landing's failed takeover bid of Linus Apple's company. When Joss, via Harris, offered to buy the Linus Apple estate and explained to them his unique reason, their interest was piqued. And now, apparently, it was a done deal.

"Nothing brings people closer together than a common enemy," Joss typed.

"So the house is yours, my friend," Harris typed back. "With all of the already agreed upon provisions intact. The papers are on their way."

Harris brokered a deal that bought Joss the Linus Apple Estate as-is, with everything in place--even the staff. He arranged to move in the following week, since he would be bringing very little with him. And most of the contents of the house were just on loan, as part of the complicated buy/lease agreement that came with the house. There were billions in art and antiques that would remain in the house but wouldn't transfer ownership to Joss.

His first guests: Klondike and Geezer.

"That's a bloody 13th century Kamakura," Klondike frothed, looking through the glass at the Japanese Katana sword. Joss was touring him through the ancient weapons wing of the Linus Apple estate. "You can't even buy one, they're so bloody rare."

"What a little girl," Geezer chided.

Joss didn't show it well, but he was glad to see both of them. He hadn't had contact with either of them the whole time he was at his folk's house. He hadn't seen anyone except Anthony and his parents.

"This is better than the bloody Louvre, mate." Klondike fixed Joss with a look of desperate glee.

"What a wanker," Geezer remarked to Joss.

Klondike's obsession with the estate's accoutrements gave Joss and Geezer some much needed time over that weekend. "You hanging in there?" Geezer asked as they strolled the grounds.

"By a thread," Joss answered honestly. "But I was even worse before," he continued. "If I hadn't had Anthony to shake me out of it, I'd be trying to figure out what the hell I was going to do well into the next millennium."

140

"You can tell a lot about a person by who their friends are," Geezer concurred.

"I don't know." Joss looked distant. "I don't think I deserve the friends I have."

"Bollocks, you wanker," Geezer slapped him on the head.

Since moving into the old Linus Apple estate, Joss had built a daily ritual: he got dressed up, poured himself a drink, and walked to the edge of his back lawn. There was a dock extending from his backyard into Lake Agave. He stood at the edge of it and looked out into the water, across and over to East Agave, to the house just on the other side from his.

He brought Geezer out there, on the final night of their visit. It was so damn big, Geezer thought as he stared at the Graft house, a bigger-than-life-size replica. It was a bloody American horror story. A *haunted* house, filled with something far older than its inhabitants.

"Feels like you can almost touch it," Geezer said to Joss, looking across the water from the pier.

"Yeah," Joss answered, with the glazed look of an addict. He stretched out a trembling hand. "I *can* almost touch it."

CHAPTER SEVENTEEN

```
// -------------------------------------------------
----------------------------
<text.rpt>" <<<<<<<<<a>
<<<<<<<<<<<<<<<<<<<<<want to<<<<<<<<<<<<<<<<<<<<<<<
<<<<<<<<<<<<<<<<<<<<<make it fun<<<<<<<<<<<<<<<<<<<<
<<<<<<<<<<<<<<<<<<<<<don't trust<<<<<<<<<<<<<<<<<<<<
<<<<<<<<<<<<<<<<<<<<<anyone<<<<<<<<<<<<<<<<<<<<<<<<
        <c++>" a>

// -------------------------------------------------
----------------------------
```

"I just got a weird text," I said to Reed, looking up from my mobile. "I think it was from Maisey, but..."

"Well, what does it say," Reed asked impatiently.

Charlize answered, reading from the phone, "You've sent a message to a guest of the Alarcón Hotel. The Alarcón is a device free environment. Namaste."

"They're already inside," he sped up a bit. "I forgot they don't allow cell phones and gadgets. We're nearly there anyway."

"It's pretty dead down here tonight," I said, thinking about how bustling it all seemed during my daytrips with Maisey.

"It's always dead downtown at night," Reed corrected. "Which makes it the perfect location for a 24-hour party."

"I hope we don't actually have to *stay there* 24-hours," I joked, turning towards Reed.

"Oh, yes we do," he turned to me with a bullyish grin. "It's in the contract. Charlie, didn't you read about this? I mean I thought you were hip on all the cool things."

"I guess I missed this one."

"Wait. Are you talking about Kool-Aid?" Charlize piped up.

I looked at her sideways.

"Yes, ma'am..." Reed nodded, making a turn into a parking garage.

"You've gotta be shitting me." She sounded skeptical.

"No shitting involved," Reed remarked. "Unless that's what you're into."

"You have tickets?" Charlize seemed baffled at the notion.

"What's the big deal?" I asked.

"It's Burning Man for rich people." She looked at Reed. "For *really* rich people."

Reed made a mocking gesture.

"The tickets are fifteen thousand face value," she said, derisively. "And there were some going on eBay for well over fifty."

I don't have to ask Charlize how she knows about all this. Especially since somehow Reed knows. I guess living in the cocoon of Agave had eroded my social awareness.

"The price makes it exclusive," he sneered. "They don't want just anyone coming to a party like this."

I looked at Charlize and she gave me the vomit sign.

"I had to pay for that one. But she's worth it, I'm sure." Reed's sardonic smile took up the whole rearview mirror.

"Screw that," Charlize shot back at Reed. "I don't need any favors. Especially not expensive ones," she said, appalled. "I don't even want to be around the kind of people who'd pay that." She turned to me, "Sorry, Charlie. You can call me tomorrow," she gave me a peck on the cheek.

"Wait," I tried to say to her, but the word couldn't seem to find its way out.

We got out and I felt lightheaded, about to pass out. I grabbed onto the side of the car for support and took a few deep breaths. I don't usually get carsick, but my head was swimming.

"Ms. Angel, is it?" Reed said to Charlize, handing the keys to a valet.

I was about to faint, my vision blurred.

They both turned to look at me. Charlize tried not to crack a smile.

"He's going to need you." Reed looked at her soberly. "Starting right about..." he checked his watch. "Now."

She looked at Reed, puzzled.

"We had some appetizers earlier this evening," Reed explained. "Which should be starting to kick in."

She stared at him trying to decipher what he'd just said, and then put it together. There was a pregnant pause. I was having trouble figuring out what the hell they were talking about. My head felt like it was the size of a hot air balloon. I remember Charlize looking at me as if she'd just discovered something very important that pertained directly to me.

"You dosed him..."

Reed just grinned.

"What is this secret communication?" I asked them, but the words slurred. "Why are you speaking in code? Are you spies?"

"And he doesn't know?" She looked at me with a clear bit of worry and concern in her eyes.

"Nope," Reed smiled, laughing at me. "Not yet, at least."

I lost my ability to focus on what they were saying. It just sounded like muted garble to me. Then I realized I had my hands over my ears.

"Charlie?" I could see Charlize's lips moving as she approached me.

Whatever sounds she was making just reverberated and trailed-off. Everything was slow and muted but bright and colorful at the same time. Hmmm, I thought, as I stared at my left hand, which almost seemed transparent. That's weird.

I suddenly had the most deep and profound appreciation for everything. The kind you feel when you've been drinking, but multiplied times ten.

"Charlie?" Charlize was right in front of me now, but she sounded distant. "Charlie, honey, answer me."

She gently took my hands away from my ears. "Drink this." She handed me a bottle of water and I just stared at it for several seconds.

I thought to myself how amazing water is, just the idea of it.

"Isn't it amazing,?" I said to them.

"Yes," Reed said to me. "It really is."

"This isn't funny," she barked at him. "He could OD or something."

"Nope," Reed said, holding a hand up in the air. "Not this stuff. C42 or something…"

"C_4?"

"That's it."

"You have C_4?" she asked in an almost lustful tone.

"Bartender," I said to one of the parking attendants, who looked at me like I was an alien. "Give her one of whatever I'm having."

"Do you want some?" Reed asked Charlize, in a mocking tone.

She thought about it for a few seconds—a drug with absolutely no side effects, but each dose is a hundred thousand dollars. She shook her head but then hesitated, looking at Charlie and then Reed and then at the doors of the Alarcón.

"No." She looked back at me and sighed. "But I want to stay with Charlie."

"Deal." Reed extended his hand to shake. "We can even say that is how you earned your ticket. So you don't think of it as charity."

146

"I'll take care of him." She turned to Reed, ignoring his outstretched hand. "But I'm *not* taking care of you."

Reed smirked haughtily. "I can take care of myself, little lady."

I looked up at her; the phosphorescence of the parking lot gave her a diamond star halo. "You're the most beautiful thing there ever was." I started to tear up. "Or ever will be."

"He'll normalize in an hour or so," Reed told her. "And then it's smooth sailing for the next twelve hours. Apparently it's a very clear high. Ultra-clear. They say you wouldn't even know you were on anything, but for the fact that you feel like a superhero."

"Please just stop talking," she said without turning back to him.

She smiled at me and gently stroked the side of my face. It felt like she was breathing life and love directly into my body.

"Thank you," I said to her. "Thank you for everything."

"You're quite welcome, sugar."

She put my head in her lap and gently stroked my hair. It felt like she was spinning gold out of it.

"How do you do that," I asked her, laying on the steps leading into the hotel.

"I don't know," she said.

"Can you do it forever."

"I'll try."

"Let's go inside," Reed whined.

"You go. Please." Charlize ordered him, still cradling my head in her lap. "Charlie and I will wait here until he feels up to it."

Reed tossed the tickets to her and they fell to the ground. She looked up at him in utter disdain and Reed just gave a dull smile in return.

"Might want to hang onto those," he said, as he made his way through a revolving door marked ONE WAY.

I don't really recall much of that first hour that I spent getting acquainted with C_4. Except that I was nestled in the loving arms of Charlize just outside the Hotel Alarcón.

I had taken a hit or two off a joint my junior year and that had been more than enough to last me the rest of my life. I remember hiding in the attic of whoever's house party I was at. I spent the rest of the night up there, engaged in a long conversation with my dead relatives, which I can't remember a word of to this day.

Life always held enough introspective moments for me that I never felt the need for any supplements. And to my surprise, Charlize hadn't gone beyond casual experimentation either. But she knew what to do. Enough of her friends partied and ultimately crashed into flames that she sort of became the Florence Nightingale of the Mission district: always there to help her wayward friends with a safe place to come back to Earth.

But C_4 was another story. Rumored to have been created in a lab at an undisclosed location in Silicon Valley, C_4 was the only known hallucinogen to not have any ill or damaging side effects. It was the wonderdrug of the wunderkind. Most people who had heard of it thought it was just a fable; that it didn't really exist. And given its price tag and limited availability, there had been very few people who had any direct encounter with it. I assume its outrageous cost and exclusivity was the only reason it ended up on Reed's radar at all. He was always more comfortable with the security blanket of his Vodka Tonic. Of course, that night he had something to prove. Just what exactly that was I still don't really know. Then again I probably do.

I remember yawning for what seemed like five straight minutes, and then when I was finished everything came into a sharp focus. A clarity I hadn't known was even possible. I looked at Charlize and her face was like a painting: colors danced and swirled and kindness and beauty radiated from her pores.

There was a light. The light was like a secret language that I could understand as if it had been my mother tongue. I knew everything Charlize was thinking without her even speaking a word of it. "I'm glad I found you too," I said to her. "And you don't need to worry about me. I'm not like them."

At first she looked at me with mild shock, trying to piece together how I had answered her thoughts as if she said them out loud.

"I know," she confided. "I'm just letting out all my anxieties now, before we go in."

"Yeah," I agreed. "Probably a good idea. Can't you hear that?" I asked craning my neck toward the revolving door.

"The music," she asked, listening for it. "Not yet."

"Not the music," I smiled. "The voices. Everyone's so busy with their thoughts that they're missing the point. It's psychic anarchy in there."

Charlize laughed and brushed my cheek. "Well, for tonight, you're the point of it all. For me at least." She kissed my forehead.

"You've been so many people," I said to her with naked emotion. "But they haven't been you."

"We're gonna have to write all this stuff down and save it so you can tell me what it all means some time."

"It's already recorded," I said, pointing toward my head. "I've got it," I smiled. "I've got it."

I got to my feet and had to adjust to the change in altitude.

"Are you all right?" she asked. "Sure you don't want to sit down a bit more before..."

"No," I said, breathing in the air of the parking garage like it was a rose garden. "I'm just so damn tall," I said, in wonder. "How did that happen," I asked her.

"All those Midwest meat and potatoes," she teased.

"Of course," I said, laughing. "That's right, I forgot."

"Oh, Charlie," she said shaking her head grinning. "Are you sure you want to go in there. We could just go back to my place and forget these losers."

"Yes," I said. "We could."

"Alright then," she said, perking up. "Let's do it."

Why couldn't we? I thought. There was a reason.

"No... wait," I blinked as if trying to tune my head to a different frequency. "I forgot." A wave of sadness passed over like one of those rainclouds that comes from out of nowhere. "We can't leave Maisey and Joss."

"Your cousin?" she asked, clearly disappointed.

"Yes. They're in love."

It was almost as if I could see them: fugitives on the run, from what they were running after. The villain wasn't just a person; it was an idea. It was the past.

"We have to save them, help them escape." I was beginning to gain my bearings. "There's a war going on."

Charlize looked as if she were a fortuneteller trying to read a crystal ball. I was the ball though, and I don't think I was very clear to anyone looking at me from the outside.

"I'm sorry. Why don't you come inside," I said, pointing to my head. "It's a lot easier to tell what's going on from in here."

She looked deeply into my eyes and smiled in recognition of what she saw.

What?" she asked cautiously.

"We've been on our way to each other forever," I said with absolute certainty. "Don't you remember?"

"Remind me."

I took Charlize in my arms and brushed my lips gently across her neck, taking in the salty taste and sweet caramel of her skin. And when my lips slowly made their way to hers, after exploring every drop of skin along the way, we fell into a feeling deeper than sleep, or maybe even death. "That's who we were," I whisper. "This is who we are."

"Uh-huh," she said between the folds of a warm, soft kiss. "If you say so."

"I do."

$$$

A couple days before that fateful night at the Hotel Alarcón, Joss drove me to the city. He had a lunch meeting with Harris Fink. And while he gave no sign of it, I could tell that Joss was sensing a close to the matters at hand, or at least a breaking away from where things had come together.

"Holy shitballs, Joss," Harris bellowed across the main dining room of the Four Seasons.

The mostly older and uptight patrons of the Four Seasons hotel looked up from their fine china and crystal goblets to stare incredulously at Harris, who was still exhaling pot smoke from the joint the maître d' had made him extinguish.

"You look better than I've ever seen you," he exclaimed. "What are you on?" He asked in a hyper-inquisitive basso.

"True love," Joss smiled, getting up to prepare himself for the imminent bear hug he had come to expect.

"Well, it suits you," Harris said.

After Harris released Joss from the massive embrace, we were introduced.

"Get up," Harris barked at me.

You could see the wait staff, anxiously eyeing the other diners who were all fixed on our party, as if we were the floorshow—shaking their heads in firm disapproval. I awkwardly shot up from my chair as if I were being summoned at gunpoint, and Fink wrapped his meaty arms around me, pulling me in as if I were his long lost brother. The soft silk wrinkles of his black suit wreaked of incense and pot smoke as he pressed me so deep into his chest that I was sure I was gonna get a contact high.

"I've heard good things, Charlie," Harris whispered loudly into my ear. "Thank you for being there for our boy." We sat down at the table again, and Harris waved at the gawking diners as if he were about to take an intermission. "The next show is at 3:00," he announced, before falling into his chair. "Hope you can make it."

"Thanks for coming, my friend" Joss said, as the drinks came.

"Please." Harris waved his hand. "I've been trying to get you up here forever. I'm sorry I haven't visited yet," Harris said with genuine regret. "I spent a lot of time in Linus' house over the years but I just can't stomach going down to the Valley these days. It's so fucking corrupt."

Joss laughed.

"The wrong kind of corrupt, I should say," Harris added, with a sinister wink.

"So, is everything taken care of?" Joss looked at Harris soberly.

"Yes. We moved all the accounts and removed you from the company charter." He eyed Joss reticently. "Are you sure this is what you want to do?"

"It's what I have to do." Joss looked at me with a sincere smile. "You never know when you might need to escape from it all."

"Believe me," Harris agreed. "You know what I've been telling you all along."

"It's far more important to know when to get out, than when to get in," Joss replied.

"Grasshopper," Fink exclaimed, mussing up Joss' hair then turning to me. "He's my finest student," he gushed, pride coming out of his pores.

"I owe you so much," Joss said, with deep appreciation. "And you're gonna take care of Charlie here?" Joss gestured to me with a wink.

"Charlie is already taken care of," Harris affirmed.

"What do you mean," I asked.

Harris started to explain, but Joss cut him off. "Never mind that now, Charlie." Joss nodded.

"But I don't need anything..."

"Please, Charlie." Joss smiled, with a hint of sadness in his eyes. "Just let me do what I do. Don't ask questions or argue with this part of it."

"But I don't even know what you guys are taking about," I said, with a puzzled expression.

"If something happens... if I have to go away. If Maisey and I have to go away... I need to know everyone in my life is taken care of."

"What do you mean, 'go away'?" I demanded.

"There's no need to delve into things that probably won't even occur," he said with a comforting smile. "If there's one thing I've learned," he glanced toward Harris, "it's that it's better to prepare for the unexpected."

"Because the unexpected is always preparing for you," Harris chimed in.

CHAPTER EIGHTEEN

The company that created C₄ had purchased an old-fashioned hotel called The Alarcón, which had been shut down fifty years ago and left to rot. They spent the last year pumping in an estimated 3 billion dollars, turning it into a boutique for the ultra rich and famous. The rumor was once the FDA approved C₄ they would have drug resorts popping up all across the globe.

The clandestine hotel project was still under construction and encased in an outer layer to keep the weather and the public out. This was the first time its doors opened—to a select group of ticketholders that looked less like Burning Man attendees and more like Willy Wonka or the Great Gatsby as re-imagined by Lady Gaga. An amalgamation of styles and eras and hopes and dreams all blended into a psychedelic Petri dish that took the science of excess to a whole new level of game.

As soon as Charlize and I walked through the revolving door, into a small room off the parking garage, all of the lights started screaming at me that there was just way too much. "Turn back," they said. But I couldn't. Even though I believed them.

A handsome, well-dressed man approached us as we entered. "I'm Philip," he said, cheerfully approaching us with a silver tray. "I'll be taking your tickets and all electronic devices." Philip was dressed in a perfect black tuxedo, cut like a knife, with an eerie set of feral horns protruding roughly from his forehead. "Leave your demons at the door," he smiled, pointing to a sign. NO DEVICES ALLOWED WITHIN THE HOTEL. "Cameras too."

Charlize and I fished for our cells and placed them on the tray. I couldn't seem to execute this simple action in the altered state I was in, so Charlize helped me out.

"Your tickets?" He said it politely, fixing his fiendish bloodied eyes on me. Contacts, I hoped.

"Here." Charlize placed them on the tray next to our phones

Philip noticed me staring at his horns. "You like them?"

"Uh, yeah," I stammered. "They look real."

"They are real." He smiled proudly. "Or at least permanent."

"You had them... implanted?"

"Yes," he said, enthusiastically. "Isn't it just wonderful?"

"I didn't know you could do that," I said. What I was really thinking was why would you *want* to do that.

"You can do just about anything," he said with a dirty grin. "You want to touch them."

"No," I said. "Definitely not."

A picture-perfect Goth chick came out of one of the doors, like something out of a Tim Burton movie. Philip gave her his tray and came back to us with another. It had two blue pills and two cups of water. "No thanks," Charlize said for the both of us. "We already took the red ones."

"I'm afraid it's mandatory," he nodded. "Don't worry, though, it is not a drug. Nothing more than a nanochip with a laxative-based delivery solution. It will serve as a locating device should any medical, or other, emergencies arise. It's necessary for insurance purposes and was mentioned several times in your ticket contract."

"You want us to swallow tracking devices?" Charlize looked at him incredulously.

"They are completely harmless and will exit upon your next discharge," he assured her. "There are strict regulations with these things." He smiled. "Plus it discourages anyone from making a break for it."

My next discharge? I thought, wincing. Charlize looked at me and I shrugged my shoulders.

"Charlie." Charlize searched my eyes. "This is getting weird. And my threshold of weird is pretty high."

The doors opened automatically after we both took the blue pill. Light and sound came flooding into the white room, drenching the walls around us. Deep purple bass and swirling colors. Philip gently prodded us forward, and whispered: "See you in the afterlife."

Before I could turn back we were sucked into a cavernous ultra lounge at the base of a ten-story spiral of people dancing like they were on fire. I grabbed Charlize's hand and we looked at each other wordlessly. The whole hotel was in the shape of a massive erect tube. The air was thick with shifting colors as if we were inside a giant lava lamp. Or a bong. There were a few thousand people, I guessed. Endless bodies, pulsating in time to the rhythmic bass, some on the dance floor some hanging over the rising circular walkways corkscrewing up the ten-story silo. There were three DJ's revolving around the center of the atrium, suspended above the crowded dance floor, battling each other. You couldn't tell how exactly they were hovering there. But simple matters such as gravity had ceased being a concern for me.

"They can't all be billionaires," Charlize commented, looking at the teeming leagues of partygoers coating almost every surface of the hotel.

"Maybe not, but all of them are quite definitely on C$_4$," I added.

"Except me," she said, transfixed by the carnal display on every floor of the building, rings of fire rising up ten stories.

There was something unsettling about the décor—statues of Hindu Gods, along with sacred tapestries from Mesopotamia and chunks of brick and mortar from the Great Wall of China. Cultural riches of untold worth gaudily strung together like a rich kid's friendship bracelet.

"Holy shit." Charlize turned to me. "What have we got ourselves into?"

I worshipped the fact that she said *we*. "I know," I answered. "This is what it looks like when someone vomits money."

We made our way to a railing looking over the dance floor. A lavender mist crept across the dance floor and wisped its way up to us. There was a pit of dancing, bobbing bodies crowded pulsating around the center. And there was Maisey at the heart of it. She was on top of an impossibly large Grand piano surrounded by a small armada of men who were doing back flips and somersaults in time to the beat of the music. Everyone in the packed room seemed to be cheering them on.

Charlize turned to me, "Is that?" I could tell she knew it was Maisey, even though she'd never laid eyes on her.

"It most certainly is."

And then Maisey looked over at Charlize and I as if we had a neon sign pointing at us. "Charlie Middle," she belted out. "You came for me!"

Beyond all laws of physics her words traveled right to us through the impossible noise. She blew me a kiss and the crowd that was surrounding her turned to look at us like we were part of the show. Clearly Maisey had taken to the C4, which was in the champagne that we toasted with back at the Graft estate. I had expected Joss and her to freak out a bit, maybe even go on the attack once they figured it out. I didn't see Joss around. But Maisey sure didn't look all that put out. Of course, it felt almost chemically impossible to freak out at the moment. Everything was far too perfect to freak out.

"Looks like you made it after all, *Old Sport*." Joss' voice came from behind me, in an effective enough Reed impression to make me do a double take.

"I'm so glad to see you," I said, wrapping my arms around him, unsure of how okay he really was.

"There you go now, Charlie Boy," he said laughing. "What? Did you think we'd made a run for it? We probably should have." He looked down and was silent for a second. "Quite a trick our old chum pulled." He smirked bitterly.

"Where is he?" I asked.

"He darted upstairs as soon as he got here. He saw me, though. My mind is going a million miles an hour, Charlie."

"That's funny," I smiled. "Mine isn't moving at all."

Charlize cleared her throat. "Oh, I'm sorry." I blushed. "Joss, this is Charlize."

Joss gave an impish smile, took her hand and gave it a tender kiss.

"Good to meet you, Joss," Charlize said with an appraising smile. "You have quite a friend here." She gestured toward me.

"That I do," he said sincerely, and in that moment all of the fractured light dancing around his head abated. Joss and I turned back toward Maisey, who was still going at it.

"I thought you'd be pissed off," I said to him, as we watched her dancing on the piano like she was in some acid drenched musical from the forties.

"It's quite beyond that, isn't it," he said, in a calm and sturdy voice.

"Really," I said, skeptically.

"All's fair in love and war. Right?" He grinned.

"Especially when you're dealing with both." I searched the room for any signs of Reed.

"You guys talk like you're in a foreign movie," Charlize remarked.

"We are," Joss smiled. "But I think the C_4 provides the subtitles."

As if on cue, the muscle-bound men in multi-patterned tuxedoes lifted Maisey up, handing her from one set of arms to the next, in one well-choreographed swoop, until her feet landed effortlessly on the red velvet carpet amidst the swarming crowd. The whole operation gave the illusion of flight. Cheers went up and Maisey took a graceful bow then made her way over to us. A path cleared for her at every step, as if she were Moses in high heels. As she approached, I could feel Joss begin to swirl and I could sense the cacophony in his head.

"You don't have to go through with it," I whispered to him. "You know that, right?"

He looked at me with his last bit of clarity. "I wouldn't know the way back if I tried."

"Charlie Middle, has it come to this?" Maisey had made her way up through the glittering mob to the waterbed couches we had scored. She ran a finger along Joss' chest and stood in front of Charlize, looking at me. "You've found someone else?"

"It couldn't be helped." I winked at her.

Maisey released me and took hold of a stunned Charlize. "You are an absolute dream," she said, looking her up and down. "Have you fallen in love with my Charlie Middle yet?"

"Well…" Charlize was shell-shocked, her eyes darting to mine for support, "we did just meet."

"You don't even have to meet Charlie Middle to fall completely in love with him."

"She's still in the grace period," I spoke up.

"Of course she is," Maisey sighed dramatically. "All the flags will fly tomorrow, though, in all the countries around the world who still believe in love." She took my face in her hands.

Maisey wrapped herself around Joss' arm and you could see his whole soul inflate as he pulled her close.

"That was pretty impressive." Charlize gestured to the piano where the tuxedoed men that were surrounding Maisey were now doing some pretty daring acrobatics.

"Oh, I just love Russian men." She feigned a swoon. "Those are the Rudanskyas, sons of the Russian oligarch. They formed a dance company in Moscow, but their father was so embarrassed he threatened to disown them if they didn't leave Russia. So they ended up here."

161

"Are they the one's who…" Charlize started.

"Yes, Dancetoyefsky," Maisey interrupted. "The Russian Cirque Du Soleil."

"I don't want to spoil the mood here," I interject. "But I think it would be a good idea if we got the hell out of Dodge."

"Whatever do you mean?" she exclaimed, as if I had said we were cancelling Christmas. "Hide! Charlie Middle, you must be crazy. I forbid it. I absolutely forbid it."

I glanced at Charlize, who was sinking into a sullen posture.

"Arcn't you concerned with what Reed might have planned?"

"He can't do anything," Maisey scoffed. "It's too late for him, Charlie. He might have been human at one point." she stared off dreamily for a moment, then caught herself. "But it's all over now."

I looked at Joss and he just nodded approvingly. It sort of made me want to strangle him.

"He drugged us, Maisey," I pleaded. "You don't think… I mean do you really believe he's gonna give up without a fight," I warned. "You heard him. 'To the winner go the spoils.'"

"Let him have his spoils," she declared with an unconvincing wave of her hand.

"You don't get it," I said, to her rolling eyes. "You *are* the spoils. And I don't think he cares if the spoils are destroyed or lost," I added gravely. "As long as he wins."

Maisey broke away. "The person I'm most concerned about isn't in this hotel tonight." An unsettled pall settled over her.

"Your father can only do so much. Reed's actually here; he's in the building."

"Oh, Charlie Middle," she sighed. "You *really* haven't figured it all out yet, have you?"

I stared at her for a few seconds then darted nervously at Joss and then Charlize. A chill ran up my spine and I felt like lightning was about to come out my fingertips. Was I missing something?

"Reed is nothing but a pawn in my father's game." She laughed bitterly.

I glanced at Joss who had a battle-hardened look on his face.

"Do you really think it's Reed you're rescuing me from?" She smiled at me like I was a child. And a lot of me still was. "Charlie Middle—my sweet, sweet boy—I'm afraid you've brought a knife to a gunfight."

I paused with that, and considered how I had been focused on Reed. While he was dangerous, he wasn't deadly. It occurred to me in that instant, that there is a difference.

"Well, here we all are!" A voice rumbled from behind us. "Back together like one big happy family."

Reed popped up out of the crowd like a wayward buoy and we all startled in unison.

"Aren't you glad, now, you decided to trust me?" He held his arms wide as if ready for a group hug. Drink in one hand, cigar in the other.

"I wouldn't say trust now, Old Sport." Joss was still, but he foamed just below the surface.

"How's that," Reed asked, half the smile being wiped from his face.

Joss seemed to lean forward toward Reed and I got a shot of nerves. I thought about the two of them in a fight. Reed looked twice Joss' size right now, and he manhandled horses and all that. I got a sick feeling in my stomach and fingertips.

"Joss, no." I couldn't even hear if I had even said the words.

Charlize reflexively grabbed on to me.

"You really do have pretty low self-esteem," Joss continued as Reed looked on, unblinking. "To pull a sad stunt like that."

Maisey was no longer clutching Joss' arm. She looked lost and confused. Reed gave her a long deep regard. "I'd say I've been rather hospitable, given the circumstances. Besides," Reed said with a crooked smile, turning back to meet Joss' smoldering stare. "You'll never have her."

Joss seemed to edge even closer toward Reed and I reflexively reached for him. He swatted my hand away.

"Oh, *I* won't stop you," Reed chuckled. "No." He glanced at Maisey who wouldn't meet his gaze. "She'll decide all on her own."

"Stop it, the both of you!" She let out a cracked plea, looking deathly pale all of a sudden.

I could see Joss twitch and knew that he was about to break. I could feel the C4 kicking into a violent place; it had found a stitch somewhere in Joss and Reed and was preparing to unravel it.

Joss made a forward motion and Reed steadied himself as if preparing to counter.

"Nooooo!" Maisey screamed at the top of her lungs. It broke the tension like a chandelier dropping onto a glass floor. "Damn you both," she spit, and broke through the crowd, toward the stairs.

Everyone around us gawked like psychedelic tourists at a crime scene. Joss made to follow Maisey but Reed lunged and tackled him. They both went down hard.

"What the fuck," I yelled, all of a sudden turbo-charged and rushing at Reed.

Before I got two steps a giant set of gorilla arms wrapped around me. I was wrapped into a chokehold and forced to the ground. There were screams from the crowd and a bloodthirsty vibe began creeping up through the C_4 haze. Out of the corner of my eye I saw Joss kick at Reed, making contact with his shoulder. Reed buckled and a security guard pounced on him. Joss wriggled away through the crowd, evading a third security guard, and ran after Maisey.

"Get off him!" I heard Charlize plead to the security guard pinning me down. "He was trying to stop the fight, you primate!"

"It's okay," I said, in a compressed muffled-breath as the rent-a-marine secured me with a plastic band, ignoring her pleas. "They got away."

It occurred to me, even in that moment: you can win the battle and still lose the war.

```
//======================99==========================
 yea // DropDownButton

     IBOutlet though i drive DropDownButton

             *dropDownButton;
}
         {through} the valley of death===
@property (copy) IBOutlet NSMenu *buttonMenu;

// the action methods for all the buttons:

             //i shall fear no evil :(id)sender;
- (IBAction)pullsDownAction:(id)sender;
- (IBAction)popupAction:(id)sender;

//===================))00=========================
```

Joss had caught up to Maisey when she couldn't get past the main door.

"I want to go home," she cried, banging ceaselessly on the door. "I don't want to go back. I want to be asleep, alone at home. Please." She was huddled on the floor, inconsolable.

Joss bent down to hold her and she socked him in the stomach. "Don't you see what you're doing here! What I'm doing here?"

A man the size of a professional wrestler, wearing a perfectly tailored suit, was towering over Joss. "I'm going to have to ask you two to come with us." He had a couple other glandular-rich clones beside him. The main guy wore a nametag that said Ben. They all had those little ear things like the FBI use.

"The young lady needs to leave." Joss stood up tall, and came right about to Ben's chest.

"I'm afraid the ticket contract states that you have to be here until at least noon tomorrow, sir," Ben droned, as if he'd repeated these words more than once tonight. "We have facilities upstairs if you need to be alone or need medical attention. Please follow me. Right now." Ben's meaty paws lifted Joss by the back of his coat as if he were a rag doll.

In a fit of desperation Joss blurted out the only thing that came to mind: "Harris Fink!"

The men froze. Ben reflexively let go of Joss. "Are you... are you guests of Mr. Fink," Ben blinked.

"Uh, yes," Joss lied, trying to gain composure.

Ben put a hand to his earpiece and muttered something unintelligible. Joss realized that dropping Harris' name was a bit like Russian roulette. You never knew if you'd get the best seat in the house or if you'd end up bloody and soiled in some back alley. After several tense seconds Ben looked at Joss. "What's your name?"

"Joss... Joss Stember."

Ben muttered, "Joss Stember," into his radio along with a few, short unintelligible words that might have been "and some girl," or "cinnamon swirl." Joss could hear the violent crackle of communication coming through Ben's earpiece, which meant that whoever's voice was coming out of the earbud was louder than humanly possible. You could see Ben shrink and reach to pull it out as he looked at Joss in alarm. "Yes, sir, right away." Ben attempted to recall his poise, glancing nervously at his minions. "I humbly apologize for the confusion."

"No, man," Joss said, feeling a bit guilty. "You couldn't have known."

Ben gave a slight, courteous nod. "Mr. Fink is indisposed at the moment but he *suggested* I take care of you and get you whatever you want until he arrives."

"I want to leave, with this young lady," Joss said with a firm, yet polite, demand.

"I'm sorry, sir, but I..." Ben broke off, doing the math in his head: would it be worse to call Harris back and bother him yet again or find a way for Maisey and Joss to get out of there. "Let's try the back stairs," Ben muttered, with a look that said *I'm too old for this shit.*

Joss helped a wordless Maisey along the corridors through a series of backdoors as Ben punched in key code after key code.

"Hold up," Ben stopped, staring at Joss with a sideways look. The rest of the entourage halted. Ben searched Joss' face then nodded his head and smiled. He turned to his underlings. "This is the crazy ass white-boy." His minions looked a little puzzled. "The dude who invented Remake and pulled a Houdini."

The other two yeti-sized escorts tilted their heads, as if to get Joss from a different angle, and said "No shit?" in unison. "Right on, my man." They offered their hands one at a time, executing a complex series of geometric handshakes that Joss couldn't quite execute.

"Where were you the whole time?" asked one of Ben's unnamed cohorts.

"You don't want to know," Joss answered.

Maisey perked up slightly.

"Of course we do, man," Ben prodded.

Joss shook his head nervously, glancing away.

168

"No really," Ben added. "We had a betting pool going last Christmas. I had Tierra Del Fuego. Chip here had that Moon Station that the Google dude owns." Joss thought about how the name Chip didn't exactly match the imposing figure to his left.

Maisey looked up at him, flatly, as if demanding that Joss answer.

"Home," Joss mumbled.

Ben looked confused.

"I was at my parents' house the whole time," Joss mumbled.

They all stared at him like he was speaking Swahili. "That wasn't even *on* the betting pool," Chip remarked, as if Joss must be mistaken.

"That was sort of the point," Joss said, with wilting pride.

There was an uncomfortable silence.

"I get it." Chip exclaimed. "There ain't nowhere I feel more comfortable than my momz's kitchen, with her cooking me up some potatoes au gratin and corn bread." He clicked his tongue in affirmation, as if tasting it even now.

Ben and the other behemoth looked at Chip and broke into laughter. "Now we see how you got that cute little figure of yours," Ben added, patting Chip's rather rotund belly.

Joss caught Maisey's eyes staring at him, alight for the first time since the dance floor. She quickly turned away.

"That's all right, Houdini." Ben patted Joss' back in support. "Never forget where you came from and you'll never be lost."

They pressed on, coming to a set of stairs that let them out into a fluorescent hallway with a security guard sitting on a stool at a doorway on the other end. "This is a restricted area." The redneck-looking security guard warned them, slamming down his paper in frustrated protest. "No one comes through here." He began to stand up.

"We got ya, Red," Ben said, delicately. "We don't want no troubles. My boy just needs to get his lady out."

"I'm afraid we can't allow that." The guard, awash in facial hair and tattoos, let out a sly grin as he palmed his holstered gun. "You know the rules... Tiny."

Ben looked at his colleagues. Without warning each of them drew a gun and shot the guard point blank.

There wasn't a loud crack like you'd expect, but as the beefy body of the security guard buckled and then dropped to the floor, Joss flinched. Maisey fell out of her cocooned silence and screamed. She grabbed onto Joss, who stepped up to Ben.

"This is not cool man, you can't just go around popping people!" It was the best Joss could do, given the fact that he wasn't too sure he hadn't crapped his shorts.

"Relax, Houdini," Ben said calmly, putting up his hands. "They're tranqs, he's fine." Joss had difficulty comprehending. "He ain't gonna feel nothing, and he'll be back to his beef-jerky-eatin' ass in fifteen minutes."

"Won't he... Won't he, mind?" Joss stammered, wincing at the guard's slumped body, having a hard time believing he was gonna be *fine*. "Won't he call for back up?"

Ben looked at Joss, serious as a heart attack. "He went for his gun. If he had hit you or the girl, Mr. Fink would have had our asses on a platter. Besides, we give this cracker five large and he ain't gonna complain none."

"Won't they… " Joss stammered. "Can't they track us?"

"We'll take care of it," Ben assured Joss.

"How?"

"For one thing, Mr. Fink is one of the owners of the company that makes C$_4$ That pretty much makes it his party."

Joss reeled, trying to put it together. "Of course," Joss laughed nervously. "Of course."

"There's a company that manufactures Ecstasy that is side-effect free, and you think I wouldn't be involved?" Joss could hear Harris' words now. *"Have we met?"*

After trying a few different codes, Ben stumbled onto the one that finally worked. The door opened to the lower level of the parking garage they had arrived at earlier. Ben and the gang said their goodbyes and Joss signed their ID badges as a keepsake.

He and Maisey followed Ben's directions up to the valet and managed to persuade the confused attendant to locate their keys. Joss' $500 tip probably sped that along. And before the guy with the walkie-talkie running out of the revolving door could close the gates on them, Joss and Maisey were making their way onto Battery and across Pine.

$$$

"Pull over," Maisey said, once they reached a safe distance. They were the first words she had uttered since the hallway.

"What?" Joss asked.

171

"I want to drive."

"Maisey, I don't think…"

"Please Joss," she interrupted. "I'm not asking you to think, I'm just asking you to pull over and let me drive. You've been on and on for the past however long asking what can you do for me. That's what you can do for me, Joss. Just let me drive."

Joss took a sharp breath and bit his tongue. He pulled over to the Google gas station on Market. It was in the shape of an "o." There were five other stations scattered around the different city districts shaped like a "G" an "o" a "g" an "l" and an "e." If you looked at San Francisco, or even San Jose and LA, in satellite-view on your mobile, you could see "Google" spelled out across the map.

Joss started filling up the tank, staring at the pump, which also displayed the top Google searches of the day—the clean version that is. "Money" and "Love" were the top searches. In that order. Joss trained his eyes on the spinning numbers instead of the search terms, trying to calm himself down. He was angry with her, but he couldn't quite pinpoint why. The passenger door opened and Maisey's beaded flapper costume sounded like a Latin percussion section as her legs slid out and her high heels pressed their way onto the pavement.

"I need to use the bathroom," she said, dryly. "Do you want anything?"

He just stared at the gas ticker as the gallons chased the dollars but never caught up.

$$$

"You're gonna miss the onramp," Joss said, tightly, looking the other way as Maisey unsuccessfully attempted to cut off a semi.

She let out a frustrated breath.

"This is actually the best part of the night," Joss snickered, derisively.

"Oh, really." Maisey snapped at him. "Well, let me assure you it definitely won't get any better. Certainly not for you, Joss Stember."

"Listen, we're both under the influence of a drug we don't even really understand, and that's been the least of our traumas tonight." Joss struggled to remain civil. "Let me just call us a car. It'll be here in ten minutes."

"I thought I made it clear that I needed to do something with my hands," Maisey said, coldly.

"That could be arranged," Joss smiled.

"Ugh," Maisey grimaced. "You sound like Reed."

Joss visibly buckled and started to say something but decided against it. "Fine," he said instead, turning his head out the window.

Maisey took a left and a right and another left, hoping to get back to the freeway onramp. But they ended up in a broken down alley off a street with homeless encampments on either side. "Are we even in America anymore?" She was talking to herself more than Joss.

"Right in the heart of it," Joss answered, wryly.

Maisey made a quick, desperate left, wanting to outrun this apocalyptic vision and it all happened in the blink of an eye. Joss shouted as a deep, hard thud resounded from the hood of the car—and then two more succinct thumps came from the undercarriage of the sparkling, white Maybach. Maisey braked and the car rolled forward. She braked again and finally Joss snapped out of his shock enough to pull the emergency brake and flip the shifter to neutral.

"Oh, my God," Maisey whimpered, breathlessly. "Oh, my God, Joss. What was that?"

Joss looked at her and then searched around as if trying to find his keys or his wallet. He was in a panic, but he took breaths trying to find some kind of center. He opened the passenger door and stepped out onto the dimly lit street. "Stay here, Maisey," he commanded, shutting the car door. "Lock the doors and do not get out," he shouted through the glass.

"You killed him!" A terrifying groan from the tent-filled sidewalk hit Joss in the chest.

There were swarms of ragged men and women, lining the sidewalks on either side. You couldn't tell which was which. Joss felt a lump in his chest and a drop in his stomach. The gloomy silhouettes stood there teetering on the edges of the street like a scene from a zombie movie. The streetlights lined the sidewalks like oversized gallows, every other one burnt out, casting shadows that appeared to be teeming with life. Or half-life.

Was he hallucinating this?

Joss made his way to the back of the car and saw a crumpled mass of clothes, like someone's dirty laundry had piled up too high and they decided to just leave it there in the middle of the road. It didn't move and Joss flinched as he saw a dark liquid start to leak from the bottom of the pile. Joss could hear the faint whimper of Maisey repeating her mantra from the inside of the car: "Oh, my God. Oh, my God."

"Stay in the car, Maisey," Joss shouted, eyeing the frayed, misshapen clumps of human remains now growing in number on either side of the street.

"You killed him," they kept repeating, or maybe it was just coming from inside Joss' head. He couldn't tell. But he could see that the pile of flesh and bones at his feet was no more animate than the dirty laundry it resembled. Then the first of the onlookers stepped onto the street, as if testing the water.

The solitary figure seemed to point at Joss. "You killed him."

Now they were chanting in unison, a warbled drone. A second onlooker stepped onto the street and with that it seemed that all of them started approaching.

"You killed him."

Joss eyed them nervously and stood up, wondering what the hell he was supposed to do. They seemed lifeless, bright eyes shining from burnt out husks.

"You killed him," they chanted, like the chorus of a Greek tragedy.

Joss glanced at the car and then the body, and before he knew it he was at the driver's side door screaming at Maisey. "Let me in," he shouted. "Move over and let me in!"

She looked at him. And for a heartbreaking moment Joss actually thought he saw her shake her head, as if she wasn't going to let him in. He was on his own now. But the moment passed and the door locks popped. Maisey scrambled awkwardly over to the passenger side.

"You killed him!"

Joss didn't look back, but he could feel the rank breath of the horde descend upon him. He wedged in between the open door and slammed it on someone's arm. He tried to beat back whatever it was with his left leg, but there was more than one of them trying to pry their way in. He tried to shut the door but he couldn't. A hand grabbed blindly and caught hold of his ear. Joss fumbled the shifter and pulled. He pumped the gas and the car jolted backwards, making yet another thump.

"You killed him."

He could hear the condemning groans as if they were coming from inside the car. Joss clicked the shifter again and punched the accelerator in a hopeless effort. He felt the car lunge forward. The hand that was ripping at his ear struggled to gain purchase and then was violently separated from its death grip. He felt a tear and a trickle of blood as the car veered forward. He had to swerve not to hit another darkened figure.

Joss glanced nervously at Maisey who was still repeating the words, "Oh, my God," as if it were the first time she said them. The car made a left and then a right. It was as if it was driving itself now. The sounds of sirens and visions of the undead clouded his brain and pressed down as if they were trying to suffocate him. He didn't even realize they were on the 101 South until they passed the exit to Candlestick Park. He let out a difficult breath as if he had been holding it for the last ten minutes.

Maisey looked at him. "Oh, my God, Joss." A sob began to reach out of her stunned expression and finally exploded like a grenade, shards flying everywhere, tears and razor sharp pleas emanating from her, like a Baptist preacher speaking in tongues.

The discord ping-ponged inside Joss' head until he couldn't bear it anymore and he reflexively turned the music on full blast. It was Maisey's CD she had made for him, way back when they still knew who they were. Or who they thought they were. He made to turn it off, but his shaking hands couldn't manage to reach the knob. Joss drove a steady sixty-five, his arms were rubber bands fastened to a pair of leaky water balloons; they kept slipping off the steering wheel and sending the car into sudden swerves. To the left of him, a plane went rocketing up into the night sky from SFO and Joss thought about whether they should just go straight there and board a flight to Mexico then Cuba and then some unnamed island. He kept turning around possible escape routes in his head until he was so spun out he had to pull over and puke.

Maisey was unable to get any words out except her ceaseless plea to a higher power that she didn't even believe in. It all went by in slow motion. So much so that Joss was startled when the Maybach pulled through the gates of Agave and wrapped itself around the unpaved roads, finally reaching the sanctuary of the old Linus Apple estate.

CHAPTER TWENTY

"**A** joyride ended with tragic consequences last night as a man was struck and killed and two others were injured. Vicky Varga has more on the story."

The TV startled me awake. I must have rolled over on the channel changer, which was caught somewhere beneath the Hello Kitty comforter.

"Yes, Brent, I'm standing here at the scene of last night's brutal accident in which a stolen Mercedes Maybach, worth over one million dollars, struck and killed an unidentified homeless man near the Caldecott Underpass at approximately 2:30 this morning. Witnesses say the man driving leaped out of his car and began threatening onlookers before getting back into the vehicle and running over the victim one last time. It is not being ruled as a homicide as of yet, but police are searching for a seventeen-year-old black male wearing a hoodie and sweat pants. The SFPD asks anyone with any knowledge of the suspect to call the number at the bottom of the screen. This is Vicky Varga reporting live for KFC TV News."

"Thank you, Vicky. Did you say that the car was worth over one million dollars?"

"Yes, Brent. I'm told there are only a few dozen of these particular cars in the world."

"Sounds like some body shop out there is about to hit the jackpot."

Charlize came into the bedroom, looked at the TV in disbelief and stared at me with her jaw dropped to the floor.

"Holy shit." I leapt up from her bed. "Joss and Maisey."

"Or Reed?" She added.

"No," I said. "Reed was still at the Alarcón."

I searched around Charlize's tiny apartment for my phone, upending the plush comforter and tossing her things around like they were bits of inconsequential refuse.

"Hey, hey, hey, mister!" she scolded me. "That's my stuff."

"I need to find my phone," I pleaded. "Can you call it?"

"Charlie," she said, as if talking me down from a ledge. "We left our phones at the party last night."

I suddenly recalled the dreary midmorning hours spent watching the clock tick by, waiting for the noon hour to arrive so we could finally escape the post-modern prison of the Hotel Alarcón. When the clock finally struck twelve we were so happy to be turned back into pumpkins that we rushed out without collecting our gadgets from horny Phillip and his Goth underling.

"Shit," I cursed. "Do you have a land line?"

She just laughed.

"Is there a payphone or something?" I searched around as if there might be one somewhere around her cramped studio.

"I don't think I've seen a payphone since I arrived in San Francisco, Charlie. We can use my neighbors' phone," she offered, still speaking to me the way you'd talk to a kid crying over their lost Binky.

I took hold of myself with a deep inhale and tried to eek out a rational thought.

"I can use Skype," I said to her, still fluttering with mild panic. "Can I borrow your laptop?"

"Sure," she said, reaching over to her desk and handing me the MacBook Pro.

"I have the same one," I smiled, opening it up and logging into my account.

"Well, that seals the deal then," she joked. "We truly were made for each other. You, me and 100 million other lucky shoppers."

The speakers crackled under the weight of the ring.

"Oh yeah," she remembered. "I kind of blew the speakers last week. Here," she said, handing me a set of headphones.

I plugged them in just as the call connected. "Hello?" A gruff, curious voice that I didn't immediately recognize as Joss' came through the earbuds.

"Joss?" I cried out, more dramatically than I had intended.

"Charlie, thank God," he exhaled sharply. "I've been trying to get a hold of you."

"Yeah, I'm sorry. We left our phones at the hotel." I took a breath. "I just saw the news," I added.

"We're both fine, neither of us was hurt. Where are you?" He sounded like a worried parent. "How long will it take you to get here?"

I looked at Charlize. "Do you have a car," I asked her.

She shook her head.

"Joss, I'm at Charlize's place in the Mission and we don't have a car…"

"What's the address," he asked, with business-like precision.

Charlize gave it to me and I repeated it to Joss.

"A car will be there within fifteen minutes." Something about his voice sounded wrong.

"Joss," I demanded. "Are you okay?"

He paused. "He's here."

"What?"

"Landing."

"Shit."

"He's called me in for a meeting. At his office, tonight."

"You're not going," I insisted.

"I don't have a choice." He dismissed my plea. "Charlie, I need you to take care of Maisey." I could hear him breathing impatiently. "Please."

"Of course," I said, looking up at Charlize. "We'll look out for the car."

There was a click and I pulled off the headphones. Everything was going by faster than I could keep track of, and I was worried that in the rush I might make a bad decision. "Get ready," I said to Charlize. "A car is coming to pick us up."

"Us?" she looked at me with a sympathetic gaze. "Charlie, I don't know what's going on, but it sounds like I would just be in the way. And frankly, I..."

"Charlize," I said with my heart hanging out of my chest. "Please. Come with me. I don't want to be away from you yet."

There was a swirling second where I could see her doing the emotional calculus.

"Okay, give me a minute." She darted over to the closet, grabbed some clothes and made her way through the bathroom door, stopping to stare at me before she closed it.

I met her gaze. "Thank you." I took a stuttering, weepy breath. "Just... thank you."

"You're not *nearly* as boring as your name." She gave me a sinful smile and blew me a kiss.

I watched the kiss sail over to me and fall to the floor like a stray piece of confetti.

$$$

All the hatches were battened down at the old Linus Apple estate. You could sense a bustling behind the curtain that was usually unnoticeable. I imagine this is the kind of feeling that a campaign headquarters would have on the eve of a tight race.

"She's been in there for a while." Joss was at wits' end, frantically pacing around the entryway. He was referring to Maisey, who was encamped behind the locked door of the temple that Joss had built for her.

I noticed a bandage on his ear. "Joss, what's that," I asked, pointing to his head.

"Nothing," he said, brushing me off. "I cut myself somewhere along the way." He wore a fresh suit and a clean shave, but he looked haggard.

Joss had woken up at 9am after only a few hours sleep, blurry-eyed and not quite recharged from the night's activities. It took him a few seconds to realize Maisey wasn't beside him. "At first I freaked out but Leonitus came in and let me know where she was."

"Leonitus?" I asked.

"He's my right hand man," Joss explained.

"You have a right hand man?" I said in disbelief. "Why haven't I ever seen him?" I tried to retrace the endless hours I'd spent there over the last set of weeks.

"He blends," Joss explained. "He's a xenophobe. Doesn't like to be around people, so he's learned ways around that."

"Sounds pretty detached for a right hand man," I remarked with a tinge of jealousy.

"Guys," Charlize interjected. "Are we on point here?"

"Right," Joss said, shooting her a surprised smile. "I like you." He turned to me. "Charlie, how did you..."

"Long story," I cut him off. "Continue. Please."

"There's not much more." He bowed his head in exhaustion and took a labored breath. "She won't let me in. She hasn't eaten and I think she's in shock. The only thing she'll say to me is, 'It couldn't be helped.'" He looked at me in desperation. "Do you know what that means?"

I closed my eyes, already picturing her, curled up in a fetal ball, rocking back and forth amidst the torn up shards of childhood photos and memorabilia. "Yes and no."

"I'm not sure what to do." He looked at me, as if that was my cue.

I glanced over at Charlize who was still trying to take in the magnitude of Joss' house. "Charlize hasn't eaten," I started. "Why don't you take care of her and I'll go see what I can do."

He looked at me and thought about saying something, then decided against it. Instead he nodded, as if in answer to a silent question.

"Charlize," I said timidly. She broke away from the fifty-foot Mandala-shaped ceiling, and caught my unsteady gaze. "Take care of him, if you don't mind. I'm gonna go see if I can talk down Maisey."

"You are not dull," she said in a sigh. "I'll give you that, Minnesota." Charlize and I fell into a kiss once again, until she finally pulled away. "Go on now, go fix your cousin."

The 12-foot carved wooden doors and Ivory handles that were probably made from the tusks of an actual wooly mammoth stood before me. The Church of Maisey. I approached and felt what I thought was a low hum emanating from just inside the room. As if there were monks just beyond the doors, chanting psalms from the book of Joss.

"It's Charlie." I knocked on the door lightly. "Charlie Middle." I winced, preparing for a cracked and lonely voice trapped at the bottom of a well.

"Which Charlie Middle is that now, exactly," her voice bit back. "The one that is alone, or the one with other people."

"The former, I think," I answered, trying to remember which was which. "The alone one."

The tip tap of heels on polished oak approached the door from the other side. Something metal made a sliding sound. The doors opened inward, revealing not a crumpled disheveled mess, but Maisey in all her power and glory. In mint condition.

"That's the one I wanted to see," she beamed, closing the doors behind us and securing the lock once again.

"You look much better than I had expected." I hesitated, surveying the room for signs of distress. None.

Maisey wore the flapper dress from the night before, her hair done perfectly and a soft glow about her face. She hadn't looked this well and rested since I had been in California. "I have had a revelation, Charlie Middle." She started walking across the room as she talked.

"Okay," I said, baffled.

"I spent the last several hours staring at all of these photos and clippings. These broken fragments of the past." She ran her fingers along the wall of memories. "And do you know what I saw in each and every one of them?"

After a few seconds of silence, I realized she wanted me to answer. "Yourself?" I attempted.

"No," she said, as if I had made her point. "I saw nothing, Charlie Middle. Every one of these pictures," she gestured along the wall, "has a figure in the shape of me. But they are *not* me."

I looked at her confused. "They are *of* you, though." I treaded lightly.

"I know you think I'm crazy, Charlie Middle. But I assure you I am the most sane one here." She paused, looking around the room. "There is no past," she continued. "There are only stories that we tell in the present. The past is a phantom tail that we wag, when we feel anxious; when we need to believe that we take up more space than our mere bodies occupy."

"He loves you," I said, defensively. "It's his pain, it was his way of dealing. It was all he had."

She looked at me compassionately, like I was a wounded animal. "It was his way of dealing with the past, because he couldn't deal with the present," she corrected.

"He's here now, though," I said gesturing toward the hallway. "Out that door and down those steps."

"He's not though," she wilted. "He's still in the past, Charlie Middle," she lowered her guard and I could finally see the welling of sadness behind the fervor in her eyes. "I'd like to think he could catch up to the present... But I'm not sure. In fact," she sighed. "I doubt it very much."

"He didn't tell you, did he?" She let out a piteous laugh. "Oh, Charlie Middle, how I wish I could come back. How I wish I could just be your best friend."

She ran her fingers along my arm, absently. "He's going to meet with your father, you know," I said, after too many beats of silence went by.

"I know," she said, shuttering. "I told him I wouldn't stay here if he went." She looked away, trying to hide a sudden pang of sadness.

"But he's going anyway?" I guessed.

"Yes."

186

"Maisey," I took a breath. "What are you going to do?"

"The only thing there is left to do." She stared blankly into my eyes. "Nothing."

```
// ------------------------------------------------
----------------------------
//  init.
                <level>="<"the sun also rises">
<drop>
 *placeHolder8;
                HrtIndicator      *riskBasedIndicator;

    Outlet     NSStempper                *levelSETTER;

                <level.def"
<post>


//================================================
     // DropDown

// ------------------------------------------------
----------------------------
//  initial.bware
```

Joss pulled up to the curb in front of the Sand Hill Road office of Brogan Landing. For a long minute he just sat there with his hands on the steering wheel, staring out the windshield as if it were a portal to the future. And the past. The clock on the dash said 8:55pm. And the last pink shard of the sun was reaching up into the night sky, desperately trying to hold on for just one more minute.

What are you doing? Joss asked himself. There was no answer in return.

The last time he had seen Brogan Landing in person was that fateful day nearly four years ago, right before spring was about to give itself to summer. Right before Joss was about to be handed his destiny and his walking papers.

It didn't seem like destiny now, though, as he sat in the car, alone, surveying the fractured landscape of his past, trying to find some distant ship on the horizon that was ready to take him and Maisey away from it all.

"Shit or get off the pot," he said out loud. That's what Anthony had told him.

Joss took a deep breath and opened the car door, stepping onto the pavement. He approached the imposing office building, which almost seemed to be leaning toward him, puffing out its chest, ready for a fight. A billboard, some advertisement from the Chamber of Commerce, read in big black letters:

SILICON VALLEY.
WHERE BAD IDEAS COME TO DIE.
AND GOOD ONES NEVER LEAVE.

As he approached the tinted glass doors and caught his reflection, Joss had the sensation that he was someone else at that moment. Someone he didn't recognize.

Who is Joss Stember, he thought. Is he the same kid who walked into that Malibu party and out onto the beach? Is he the same one who woke up that morning, on the sand, looking at Maisey and seeing the rest of his life suddenly come together like a kiss?

He had traded that person in two years ago. A bait and switch that he had fallen for. A bargain that ended up costing so much, despite delivering what it had promised. You can never outrace the sun, he finally understood. No matter where you are in this world, the sun has already set.

He passed through the doors of the office tower, leaving behind the doubts that he knew would be waiting for him on his way out. If he made it out.

"Sign in please." An old man who didn't even look up pushed a clipboard forward from behind an oversized podium.

Joss scribbled his name and made his way to an open elevator. He clicked the 23rd floor and as it shot up he steeled himself, refusing to let this meeting go like the last one did. The doors opened and an empty waiting room sat still, as if challenging him to make the first move. There was light leaking from a cracked set of double doors. A familiar voice escaped from beyond them. "Come on in, Joss."

Joss pushed forward, his steps heavy, and entered Brogan Landing's office.

Landing looked nearly the same. But Joss could tell that he had aged. Below the St. Tropez tan and pink cardigan that highlighted the unnatural texture and hue of his skin. Dorian Gray, Joss thought, and wondered where Landing kept his portrait.

"Sorry for the informality, I gave my secretary the night off," he winked, jovial as ever. "Have a seat, my boy."

Joss began to sit down but decided against it, conscious of every move. Not wanting to repeat the mistakes of the past. "I think I'll stand."

Landing squinted at him as if trying to get a better look. "Suit yourself, son," he said, maintaining his genial tone.

"I'm not here to listen to you," Joss said. "I'm here because I'm ready to end this bullshit game."

Landing smiled. "I see success hasn't gone to your head." He licked his lips derisively. "Taking etiquette lessons from Harris Fink, are you?"

"He's got more integrity in his little finger than you have in your whole, goddamn empire." Joss nearly spit.

Landing chuckled, "Is that so?"

"You wanted to meet with me," Joss pressed, "so here I am. Take a good look, because you won't ever see me again. We're leaving, and there's nothing you can do about it."

"Believe me, you little shit, there's nothing that pleases me more than to hear that I will never have to see you again." He picked up a burning cigar and took a casual puff. "But there's no *us*, I'm afraid."

Joss let out a breathy laugh. "Same old game, huh?" He squared his shoulders. "We're not kids anymore. You can't control us."

"I don't need to, son." He grinned in unfettered contempt. "Maisey's a big girl. She can make decisions for herself. And just like before, her decisions will not involve you. I just spoke to Reed, and to Maisey," he nodded his head. "They are reconciling as we speak." A cloud of smoke leaked from his rubbery lips and he fixed Joss with a liquid stare. "The bonds of marriage come with their own set of defenses. Protection against the interlopers that seem to crawl out of the gutters, trying to steal what isn't theirs."

"Interesting theory," Joss said, with a mocking nod. Landing stared at him, unblinking, unperturbed. "You see everything as profit or loss," Joss continued. "But not everything can be measured. Not everything can be bought. Even if you think it can."

A loud, slow clap emanated from the other side of the table. Landing's cigar that had been sticking out of his mouth tipped up as he smiled broadly. It made him look like an old carnival barker or snake oil salesman. "Very nice," Landing continued clapping, removing the cigar from his mouth and resting it in the ashtray. "Pity I don't have the security cameras turned on. You could have been nominated for that speech." Landing opened his desk drawer and pulled out a 9mm Glock.

Joss barely held back the reflex to duck and cover. "Oh, so that's what you have in mind." Joss let out a staggered breath, trying to steady himself.

"Yes, Joss." Landing smiled, checking the chamber of the gun. "That's exactly what I have in mind." He looked up at Joss, with unrestrained joviality. "Seems you can't be bought, and you've done a good job hiding your money and protecting your interests. With a crooked mentor like Fink, I'm not surprised. So, you've left me no other choice."

Joss let out a nervous laugh that died on his lips. "You can't..."

"Oh, that's the thing," Landing cut him off. "I can."

Joss started to swirl, and began to feel something leak out of him. For a moment he thought it was the last piece of the actual Joss Stember. The last little bit of holdover from what he used to be, leaving him for good. He saw his parents working eighty-hour weeks so he could afford to go to a good school. He saw Anthony sitting across from him at Tommy's Burgers. He saw Geezer and Klondike over vid chat before he had even dreamt of seeing them in person. He saw his brother laying out clothes for him to wear to the party. And then he saw Maisey, lying on the sand, just about to wake. Just about to answer Joss' latent proposal of marriage with that beautiful promise: someday.

And then suddenly he realized it wasn't a part of himself that was leaking out. No. What had been pouring out of Joss were the parts that didn't fit. The gaseous residue from the last two years: all the struggles, all the worries, the waiting. The fake memories that were now clearing the way for the real ones. Joss was letting go of the past by remembering who he used to be. By realizing that was who he still was: that same kid from before all of this began. Right here, right now.

"Joss Stember," he said to himself. "It's been a long time."

He heard a click and it was like a switch got flipped. He felt all of the energy in his body sink down into his legs; a welling strength filled him full of impossible torque. And like a catapult, Joss shot up and over the desk careening full force toward Landing's overstuffed frame.

CRACK.

Joss felt something jab into his ribs like a hot poker.

CRACK.

He felt a thud as the chair and Landing and his own body went toppling over, spilling across the white-carpeted floor.

He saw red. Then he saw white. Then he saw black.

$$\$\$\$$$

Joss awoke seconds later, blinking his eyes. He was dying. The side of his face pressed against the carpet. Landing was staring straight at him with wide, hateful unblinking eyes. Joss reflexively kicked at him, then scrambled for the gun but couldn't find it. He made as if to defend himself from an impending blow. But none came.

Landing wasn't moving. Joss stared at him and then recoiled when the crimson bubbles started oozing out of Landing's mouth.

Tentatively, Joss stuck his foot out and lifted Landing's body by the shoulder, exposing the stained carpet below. The gun was there too, Landing's fingers still clutching it tightly. A rose colored blotch was blossoming at the center of Brogan Landing's chest. Joss drew his leg away in horror and Landing's torso flopped back onto the carpet with a dull thud.

Scuttling back hastily, Joss whacked his head on the top of the large oak desk. "Oh, shit," he whispered. "Oh shit, oh shit, oh shit," he repeated breathlessly.

He got up, clutching the back of his head, looking down at his ribs where he felt a burning sensation. There was no blood. He lifted his shirt and there was a deep red mark that was quickly morphing into a full-on bruise. Joss tried to take a breath but a sharp pain from his ribs pushed it back with full force.

"No," Joss wheezed, looking at Landing.

He surveyed the room as if it could tell him what to do next. There was a security camera in the corner and Joss wondered if Landing was telling the truth about it being turned off. He'd find out soon enough. Thoughts crowded into his head jockeying for position. Should he grab the gun, should he wipe the room of prints? His name was on the register, what could he do about that? Finally, the last thought standing was: get the hell out of here. Now.

Joss ran, taking the stairs one flight at a time leaping and bounding, clutching his aching ribs. Trying to outpace the pain and the fear that seemed to be closing in like a speeding bullet. When he got to the bottom of the stairwell he put his ear to the door of the lobby, hoping to get a sense of possible danger. Nothing. He cracked the door open, and the squeak it made nearly sent him out of his skin. He stepped back, breathing heavy, before peering through.

Joss saw the old man at the podium still buried in his newspaper, not a care in the world. He took a couple of labored breaths, trying to build his courage. The door creaked again as it opened and Joss bit his lip as he made his way across the

194

lobby. He crept past the guard and had his hand on the door when he froze.

"Hold it right there," the guard commanded, in a calm but firm tenor.

Joss felt his spine unzip and his backbone turn to rubber. The wind left him and he slowly turned around, raising his hands in surrender. Oh well, Joss thought. End of the line.

"*Sign out*, please," the guard asked, in a pissy voice, without even looking up.

Joss didn't think he'd actually be able to move. Sweat poured down his face and arms. His breathing took on a life of its own and his feet seemed cemented to the floor.

The guard looked up, agitated. "Please sign out, sir."

"Yes… Yes of course," Joss stammered. He summoned every nano-ounce he could and miraculously his feet began listening to his brain. He inched over to the podium, sweat dripping onto the tile floor.

"Are you okay, sir?" The guard eyed Joss suspiciously, hand moving to the side of his hip where he must have had a gun.

"Yes." Joss was about to faint. "I'm… I'm not feeling well," Joss muttered. "Flu."

The guard took his hand from his sidearm and scooted his chair back away from Joss. "I don't need none of that," the guard shook his head. "You go along, I'll sign out for you." He looked at Joss like he was a leper.

"Thank you," Joss said with way too much feeling. "Thank you so much."

The guard pumped a wad of anti-bacterial gel into his palm and went back to his newspaper. "Goodnight," he drawled, not looking up.

"Goodnight," Joss mumbled, as he shot out the glass door and flew down the steps to his car.

CHAPTER TWENTY-TWO

"**C**harlie?"

"Joss?" I answered back.

"Where are you?" he said, short of breath.

"What do you mean?" I was lying back on my bed, staring at the ceiling tiles, hoping Charlize wasn't planning on getting dressed again when she came out of the shower.

"I thought the three of you would still be at the house," he said breathing heavy. "I'm pulling up my driveway now. Leonitus has everything ready to go. You need to get Maisey."

"Joss," I asked, trying to decipher what the hell he was on about. "Maisey said she told you she was going to leave if you went to the meeting. And, well... Charlize and I kinda wanted to be alone, if you know what I mean." I hesitated. "Wait. What do you mean, 'Leonitus has everything ready to go'? Everything ready to go for what?"

"Charlie," he gasped. "I'm in trouble."

"Joss?" I sat up in the bed.

"I don't have much time. I need to go away."

"What do you mean," I said, confused. "For how long?"

"Forever, Charlie," he answered flatly. "I need to disappear for good."

"Joss, I don't think it's that serious." I tried to calm him down. "Maisey will snap out of whatever she's going through. Why don't you just get some rest and we can talk tomorrow."

"Charlie." Joss let out a pained sigh. "I've done something... I mean I didn't actually do it, but I was involved in something."

"Joss, you're scaring me."

"I'm sorry, Charlie," he said. "You've been a much better friend than I deserved."

"Why are you talking in the past tense, Joss?" I got out of bed and staggered over to the window of the cottage.

"I'm through with the past, Charlie." Joss choked up a bit. "I just want you to know that I can never repay what you've done for me."

"Dude, are you having a weird reaction to the C4?"

"Leonitus has a package for you," Joss continued. "Which he'll deliver in the next 48 hours. Harris will also be contacting you. I tried to get it all down on my digital recorder on the way back. But, I'm sure I've left out something..."

"Joss, stop fucking around," I said, looking out the cottage window, trying to see past the trees and over the lake.

"I love you, Charlie." Joss choked up. "You're one hell of a soldier. Even in a shitty war."

"Joss!"

Dial tone.

"Shit," I said, hitting redial. It went straight to voicemail. I started getting dressed as the shower was turning off. Charlize came out drying her hair, sans any other clothes. It hurt to leave, but Joss was obviously not in his right mind. She gave me a curious and then disappointed look.

"Your cousin?" she asked, not altogether kindly.

"No," I smirked. "My king."

"Great," she sighed sarcastically. "Is this gonna be a thing?"

"I sure as hell hope not," I said, making my way over to her unchecked beauty. "You know that it physically hurts to leave, don't you?"

She wrapped the towel around her body before I could make contact. "Serves you right."

$$$

Joss hated hanging up on Charlie, but he had no choice. "Goddamnit," he said under his breath as he made his way up the front steps.

Leonitus appeared in the entryway of the Old Linus Apple estate as Joss made his way through the front door. "Go on ahead," Joss said to him. "Get the plane ready and see that everything is prepared to go. I'll be there in thirty minutes."

"Will there be one or two of you," Leonitus asked.

Joss peered over the lake to the shining mansion on the other side. He almost lifted his arms up, out of habit. But he didn't have to reach anymore, he thought. Everything was finally in his grasp. "We'll see, my friend," Joss nodded. "We'll see."

"Your injuries." Leonitus looked down toward where Joss was clutching his ribs.

"Not critical, we can deal with it on the plane." They both looked out across the darkened lake where the reflection of the Graft house was shimmering in diamonds. "Everything's on lockdown?" Joss asked, after a beat of silence.

"It's all done."

"You're gonna get this to Charlie? And everything else…"

"Of course, sir." Leonitus looked uncharacteristically ruffled. "Sir," he asked.

"Leonitus." Joss answered with a smile, shaking his head. "You cannot come with me."

"But…"

"I'm counting on you to get us out of here." Joss fixed his gaze on Leonitus. "You know there's no way you can come and have us ready to roll." Leonitus was silent. "I'll be careful."

Joss searched his pockets and patted his chest, looking for something. "Wait. You have to take the recorder." Joss took the recorder out of his breast pocket and handed it to Leonitus, then drew it back at the last second. He looked at it and pressed record.

"Dude. One last thing." He smiled as he thought of Charlie. "Hold onto that girl, Charlize. Move back to the Midwest with her. Run away," he pleaded, "as fast as you can." Joss glanced over to Leonitus, who pretended not to be watching him. He cleared his throat and continued, "It's been good to talk with you, Charlie. I'm gonna miss that more than anything. My only regret is that I didn't learn more about you. But, who knows… maybe someday we'll be on the beach of some uncharted island. And I can be the one listening to your stories."

He took a breath, trying to hold his emotions in check.

200

"Tell Maisey I love her forever, even if she doesn't decide to come with me." Joss looked across the water. "There's so much more to all this than one could ever know."

$$$

Joss pulled over to the side of the road, just short of the Graft's driveway. He exited the car and made his way stealthily along the tree line, aware that word could be out and Reed might be the wiser.

I was already on my way back over from his place by that time, having heard his engines rev from halfway along the lake path. I knew it was him and I knew where he was heading. I was a bit too hasty to get over to his place after our aborted call and now cursed myself for not driving. I started sprinting back.

Maisey and Joss had set up a signal when they first started their secret rendezvous. Joss would ring once. Then ring again. And Maisey would sneak out one of the back doors and meet him in a grove beyond the massive rose garden. They'd make love right there and lie back looking at the stars, holding on to each other for dear life.

Joss stared up at the massive house from the tree line, wondering which room she might be in at this moment. Worried she might not hear the signal. He drifted back to the first time they met. He thought of the canyon and all the people who might have gone over. On purpose or on accident.

He rang once and hung up. Then he rang again.

Maybe Joss felt like he was in high school again. He and Maisey never had the chance to play these kinds of games. They were rushed off to adulthood straightaway. Or at least some stunted version of it.

Joss made his way down the crooked path to the meeting place, the place Maisey called their "Secret Garden." A small, hidden grove tucked well behind the main garden. He came to the clearing, a weeping willow in the center and Queen Anne's lace strewn amidst the high summer grass.

"It's the most absolutely romantic place ever, Joss Stember," Maisey would always say. "I would die here if I could."

"What about just living instead," Joss would always respond.

"I'll take what I can get."

It had been twenty minutes. The crickets had begun their shrill song. The blackness had consumed the fading light. And Maisey was not going to come. Joss realized it, even if he didn't want to admit it. He had finally made it back from the past but he was too late. Tears streaked down his cheeks and his breathing shallowed. He actually didn't realize he was crying, though. Not until he heard her ask about it in that rich, raspy timbre that broke Joss' heart each time he heard it.

"Are those tears for me, Joss Stember?" Maisey's voice drifted across the thick summer air like a pair of drunken butterflies. "Or are they because of me?"

"Both," Joss said, struggling to find composure.

"Right answer," Maisey cooed, as she had the first time they met.

"I don't think I've seen you since then," he said, sniffling. "Not really anyway."

"What do you mean?" Maisey's question hovered as she drew near to Joss, who was standing underneath a willow branch.

"Maisey, I don't know what I became." He took a deep breath. "I thought I could change the way things were... so that I could be the person you wanted."

A silence passed between them.

"And I *was* able to change the way things were." He hung his head low. "But I changed who I was in the process."

"The boy I knew," she said softly.

"Yes," Joss said. "I left him back there, abandoned him."

"It appears, Mr. Stember," Maisey took him by the hands and pulled him in close, "that you decided to go back for him." She put her lips to his ear and whispered, "Do you think you could help me find the Maisey that I left behind?"

"That's why I'm here," he answered, his skin rippling and pulsing under her caress. "But we need to go," he whispered. "We need to go now, Maisey."

She pulled back a little and he held on to her tightly.

"Where exactly do we need to go?" A crease furrowed in her brow.

"Away," Joss said, breathlessly but with utter conviction. "Forever."

Maisey stepped back again, as if to get a better look at him. "What happened at the meeting Joss? What did he do to you?" A trembling fear started to surface.

Joss looked away. "He had a gun."

"Joss!" Maisey felt around his body. "Are you hurt?"

"Not badly." Joss shifted uncomfortably as her hand grazed his ribs. "But..." Joss hung his head, unable to get out the words.

"Is he—" she took a breath midsentence and a dawning realization reached her eyes. "Is he dead, Joss?" she asked in disbelief.

Joss didn't answer.

Maisey stepped back, unable to breathe. She put her hand to her mouth and started crying.

"Maisey." Joss reached for her.

"No." She put her hand up. "I'm not... Just give me a second, Joss. Please."

"Maisey, I didn't mean to do it," Joss stammered, starting to lose it. "I don't think I even did do it..."

"Oh my God, Joss." She wept, holding her hand up to her mouth. "We are cursed. We are cursed, you and I." She looked at him, shaking her head, and backed up a few more steps.

"Maisey, we have to go," Joss stood there, his arms outstretched.

She was only a few feet away but Joss could feel his grasp beginning to fail. He could feel her slipping out of reach yet again. And he redoubled his efforts.

"Maisey, I'm not going to go without you." Joss tried to grip onto her with his eyes.

"No one will be going anywhere." A voice from the darkness. Reed burst from the garden pathway. Even in the dim light they could see that he was drunk, stumbling one half step at a time toward them. He was two steps away before they saw the gun.

"Oh, Reed," Maisey sighed.

"Reed." Joss put his hands up and began inching toward Maisey. "Please, man. Don't point that at her."

"Do you really think I have no heart?!" Reed's screamed, his eyes boring into Maisey. "Do you really think that I don't hurt, that I don't matter?!" He was slurring his words.

I could hear their voices across the hedges. My feet couldn't carry me fast enough.

"You know that's not true, Reed," Maisey murmured, unable to hide her nerves.

"Reed," Joss said calmly. "Put the gun on me, Reed. Not Maisey."

I slipped through the opening and saw them there. The three of them in a crooked constellation. Joss might have caught my eye for a fraction of a second, as I tore down the garden path. But it all was happening so quickly.

"Oh, I'll do more than that!" Reed said, pointing the gun at Joss.

"Reed, no!" Maisey screamed and leaped toward Joss.

"Maisey!" Joss screamed.

I was off my feet and in the air hurling towards Reed, barreling into him with everything I had. He looked at me with the uncontrolled look of a madman, who had suddenly become sane--one split second too late.

There was a CRACK and a flash of light. And then I was still, lying on my back. The branches fluttered like birds as the fading echo of the gunshot spiraled upward. Reed had gone down and lay still like a limp dog. I looked up; the sky was missing its stars.

I was watching my life pass before me. It didn't take long. I took a deep breath, what I thought might be my last.

I looked down to get a glimpse of my wound before I went. Wait. I surveyed my body and couldn't seem to find where the bullet had entered. Couldn't find any discernable trace of a wound for that matter. I hadn't been shot at all.

With that realization, my body seemed to breathe in all the air around me and I came back to Earth. I turned and saw Maisey lying on the ground with Joss standing above her motionless. Shit.

"Joss!" I tried to shake him out of his reverie. "Goddamit," I cried out to him, frantically pointing to her limp body on the ground in front of him. "Dude, help Maisey!"

He gurgled something barely audible.

"What?" I asked, in pained frustration as I secured Reed's gun and scrambled toward the weeping Maisey.

"It couldn't be helped," he rasped.

Joss looked at me and I froze. With his whole body and soul he looked at me. He gave something to me in those few seconds that most people don't get in a lifetime. Then he looked down at Maisey. He stood there, just looking at her, almost like he was trying to reach for her but couldn't quite get his arms up. He just stood there. Gazing at her with a look of complete and absolute wonder, as if he finally understood the answer to whatever question he had been asking himself all his life. And in one broken motion he collapsed on top of her.

And then Joss Stember: kid-billionaire, mysterious recluse, star-crossed lover, and my best friend, died. Under a weeping willow amidst the Queen Anne's lace—near, if not in, his true love's arms.

CHAPTER TWENTY-THREE

```
// -----------------------------------------------------------
--
<fatal=error> ="<system crash>"

// -------------------------------------------------------
----------------------------
< (scope != NULL);="< cannot.reboot >"
// ---------------------------------------------------------
----------------------------
```

"Charlie Middle." Her voice curls around me like a hug. "My god... has it been two years?"

"Nine months, Maisey." I smile. We're sitting across from each other at a street side café in Amsterdam.

"I don't believe it." She gives me a sinful look.

"Neither do I." I bow my head in reverence.

"So where is this woman everyone keeps talking about?" She leans in, conspiratorially.

"You were there the night I met Charlize," I laugh. "You know her."

"Of course, Charlie Middle." She gives me that look, as if to say: you silly boy, just play along.

"She had a meeting at a gallery. That's why we're here. She's having an exhibit on Friday."

That's half true. We *are* here for her exhibit, but there's no meeting going on right now. Charlize just didn't want to come.

"Go Charlize!" Maisey toasts, with a sincere gesture. Our glasses clink joylessly. "I'm so pleased for you, Charlie. You do look happy. A quiet kind of happy. Which is the only tolerable kind."

We laugh for a moment, and then silence begins to brew. The weight of the object. He who shall not be named.

"Reed is good," Maisey says, out of the blue, clearing her throat.

She notices my muscles tense, a bodily gag reflex at the mention of his name. The fact that the Grafts had it written up to self-defense. The fact that Joss' name was slandered across every website and rag: THE REMURDERER. The fact that Maisey willingly and inexplicably stayed with Reed.

"So we each have someone we can't talk about," she says, in response to my terse silence.

I notice her hand absently reaching for the place on her chest where the bullet passed through, missing her heart, only to land in his. It must be a learned reflex.

"Why not just talk about *us*?" She gives me that Maisey smile, the one from the white convertible, her hair blowing as we wound in and out of traffic. The big sky. The bright lights.

The waiter brings us the third set of drinks, and we take our first sips silently.

"What is your life like now, Charlie Middle? Please tell me."

"Pretty simple," I say. "My dad wants to retire. Charlize and I are talking about taking over the hardware store from him. Other than that we hang around the house, work in the yard. I write. She paints."

Maisey takes it all in without a response. What happens beneath her smile is a mystery no man can solve. I wonder if she can even comprehend the kind of life I'm describing. I wonder if it's as foreign to her as her life was to me that summer, as her life is to me right now.

"All said, it's pretty boring." I smile, toasting her. "Which is pretty frigging awesome."

"Oh, Charlie Middle, how I envy you. I can't tell you..." she drifts off. "Well, I just can't." She gives a sad smile.

She looks at me, her face open for the first time, and then turns away. I grip on to her hands until she looks me in the eye again. "If you *ever* want to escape—" I look at her pleadingly, "there's a room open at the Stember estate."

She laughs through her tears. "Charlie Middle," she scoffs. "Would I raise your free range chickens? Or milk your cows?"

"Yes," I say with a grin. "We weren't planning on having any, but if that's what it'll take to get you there..."

"Can't you just see that?" She shakes her head in comic disbelief.

"Yes I can, actually. And it doesn't have to all be boring. Once in a blue moon, when one of us gets a wild urge for something outlandish and extravagant and impossible we can act on it. We can take Jay-Z's yacht to Cannes or grab dinner for three in the Forbidden City."

"I do believe the expression is *dinner for two*."

"Screw convention," I press on. "Stay with us here and fly back to Minneapolis. We have excess there too."

She loosens her grip and takes a breath.

"What's wrong," I ask.

"Do you know why that bullet passed through me and..."

"Maisey." I tighten my grip.

She fixes me with a ferocious gaze. There's a whirling silence as she collects herself.

"Because my heart, Charlie Middle, is three sizes too small."

She beats back a sob. I squeeze both her hands, as if somehow that will staunch the wound.

"What do I do with that?" She curses as I offer her a napkin. "How do you fix that?"

Everyone in the restaurant turns to us. I stare them down until they turn back away.

"You let it grow," I say to her, as sure of something as I've ever been.

I can see the thought hit her as she dabs at her eyes. She wipes a tear away like a stray piece of confetti and wraps her slender fingers around the stem of her glass.

I get up to go to the bathroom as she orders another drink. When I return a few minutes later she is gone. I look around but I know. My eyes fall to the table and I notice Maisey's handwriting on the back of a drink coaster.

It couldn't be helped. XO

I pick up the coaster and laugh to myself. Her lipstick mark rests underneath her words, a punctuation of sorts: sealed with a kiss. But sealed, nonetheless. That kind of sums her up:

the most introverted extrovert ever. It sums both of them up actually.

I would have enjoyed walking the cobblestone streets of Amsterdam with Joss. I deal with the fact that we had a lot to say to each other. These people in your life. Transients, but people you know you belong with. What does that mean? I feel the need to fill in the space he left with checklists. Trying to make sure I fill in every last minute. Because it could really be your last. Or your first.

Joss thought he could recreate the past. Maisey tried to outrun it. I guess my downfall is I thought I could ignore it. But the past can't be out run, or revisited. And it won't be ignored. It will just be there, pushing us back until we get beyond it.

```
// ---------------------------------------------------------------
--
<  #end
// -------------------------------------------------
---------------------------
```